The COLOR *of* HEAVEN

By
Julianne MacLean

Cover art design by Pat Ryan Graphics and The Killion Group
Photo credit: Vladimir Piskunov

ISBN: 0986842222
ISBN 13: 9780986842221

"A gem cannot be polished without friction,
nor a man perfected without adversity."

- Donina Va'a Renata

Preface

A lot goes through your mind when you're dying. What they say about life flashing before your eyes is true. You remember things from your childhood and adolescence – specific images, vivid and real, like brilliant sparks of light exploding in your brain.

Somehow you're able to comprehend the whole of your life in that single instant of reflection, as if it were a panoramic view. You have no choice but to look at your decisions and accomplishments – or lack of them – and decide for yourself if you did all that you could do.

And you panic just a little, wishing for one more chance at all the beautiful moments you didn't appreciate, or for one more day with the person you didn't love quite enough.

You also wonder in those frantic, fleeting seconds, as your spirit shoots through a dark tunnel, if heaven exists on the other side, and if so, what you will find there.

What will it look like? What color will it be?

Then you see a light – a brilliant, dazzling light – more calming and loving than any words can possibly describe, and everything finally makes sense to you. You are no longer afraid, and you know what lies ahead.

Sunshine and Rain

CHAPTER

One

In this remarkable, complex world of ours, there are certain
people who appear to lead charmed lives. They are blessed
with natural beauty, have successful and fulfilling careers.
They drive expensive cars, live in upscale neighborhoods, and are
happily married to gorgeous and brilliant spouses.

I was once one of those people. Or at least that's how I was
perceived.

Not that I hadn't endured my share of hardships. My childhood had been far from idyllic. My relationship with my father
was strained at best, and there were certain pivotal events that I
preferred to forget altogether – events that involved my mother,
which I don't really wish to go into now, but I will explain later,
I promise.

All you need to know is that for a number of years my life was
perfect, and I found more happiness than I ever dreamed possible.

My name is Sophie. I grew up in Camden, Maine, but moved to
Augusta when I was fourteen. I have one sister. Her name is Jen
and we look nothing alike. Jen is blonde and petite (she takes after
our mother), while I am tall, with dark auburn hair.

Jen was always a good girl. She did well in school and graduated with honors. She went to university on scholarship and is now a social worker in New Hampshire, where she lives with her husband, Joe, a successful contractor.

I, on the other hand, was not such a model student, nor was I an easy child to raise. I was passionate and rebellious and drove my father insane with my adventurous spirit, especially in the teen years. While Jen was quiet and bookish and liked to stay home on a Friday night, I was a party girl. By the time I reached high school, I had a steady boyfriend. His name was Kirk Duncan, and we spent most of our time at his house because his parents were divorced and never around.

Before you pass judgment, let me assure you that Kirk was a decent, sensible young man – very mature for his age – and I have no regrets about the years we spent together. He was my first love, and I knew that no matter where life took us, I would always love him.

We had a great deal in common. He was a musician and played the guitar, while I liked to sketch and write. Our artistic natures gelled beautifully, and if we hadn't been so young when we first met (I was only fifteen), we might have ended up together, married and living in the suburbs with a house full of children. But life at that age is unpredictable. It's not how things turned out.

When Kirk left Augusta to attend college in Michigan and I stayed behind to finish my last year of high school, we drifted apart. We remained friends and kept in touch for a while, but eventually he began dating another girl, and she was upset by the once-a-month letters we continued to write to each other.

We both knew it was time to cut the cord, so we did. For a long stretch I missed him – he was such a big part of my life – but

I knew it was the right thing to do. Whenever I was tempted to call him, I resisted.

I went on to study English and Philosophy at NYU, which is where I met Michael Whitman.

Michael Whitman. The name alone had a sigh attached to it…

He was handsome, charming and witty, the most perfect man I had ever seen. Every time he walked into a room, I lost my breath, as did every other hot-blooded female within a fifty-yard radius.

If only I knew then, when I was nineteen, that he would be my future husband. I probably wouldn't have believed it, but there's a lot I wouldn't have believed about the extraordinary events of my life. I doubt you'll believe them either, but I'm going to tell them to you anyway.

I'll leave it up to you to decide if they're real.

Chapter

Two

⌒⌒⌒

Michael was nothing like Kirk or any of the boys I had known in high school. His parents owned a corn farm in Iowa, but he looked as if he'd been raised by aristocrats in an English country house and had just stepped off the cover of GQ magazine.

Well-dressed and devastatingly handsome – with dark, wavy hair, pale blue eyes, and a muscular build – he had a way of making you feel as if you were the most attractive, witty, charismatic person on earth. And it wasn't just women who worshipped him. He was a man's man, too, with a number of close, loyal friends. His professors respected him. He was an A student and the class valedictorian at graduation. And then – big surprise – he went off to Harvard Law School on scholarship.

He was your basic "dreamboat," and though he spoke to me now and then on campus, like everyone else, I mostly admired him from afar.

It wasn't until four years after graduation, when I was interning in the publicity department at C.W. Fraser – a major publisher of non-fiction books and celebrity tell-alls – that I became the envy of every single young woman in Manhattan and beyond.

It was June 16, 1996. I was twenty-six years old, and had helped to organize a book launch party that Michael attended.

We saw each other from across the room and waved. Later that night, we went out to dinner, and when he escorted me home, I invited him inside. We stayed up all night, just talking on the sofa, listening to music, and we kissed when the sun came up.

It was the most magical, romantic night of my life.

One year later, we were married.

⁓

During our honeymoon in Barbados, Michael confessed something to me that he'd never been able to talk about before, not with anyone.

When he was twelve years old, his older brother Dean had died in a tractor accident. The vehicle slid down a muddy embankment, rolled over and landed on top of Dean, killing him instantly. Michael was the one who found him.

His voice shook as he described Dean's lifeless body, trapped beneath the heavy tractor.

I hadn't known about the accident when we attended university together. I don't think anyone did. Michael had always seemed so strong and dynamic. It seemed as if nothing bad could ever touch him.

As soon as I heard this, I understood that we shared something very profound – a common experience that left us both broken in unseen places, for I had lost my mother when I was fourteen.

I was still angry with her for leaving us.

Because that's what she did. She made a choice, and she left us.

I, too, shared these things with Michael, and we grew even closer.

CHAPTER

Three

⸙

When I mentioned earlier that I had once led a charmed
life, I was referring to this stretch of time, which began
on my wedding day and lasted for ten wonderful years.
Michael and I were crazy in love as newlyweds. He rose
quickly at the law firm, and we both knew it was only a matter of
time before he became a partner.

Things were going well for me, too. Six months after we
began dating, I was offered a full-time, permanent position in the
publicity department at C.W. Fraser, and with Michael's encour-
agement, I pursued my first love – writing – and began submitting stories to magazines. We dined out often and connected with
all the right people. Before long, I was leaving my job in publicity
to write for the New Yorker.

Everything seemed perfect, and it was. We made love almost
every night of the week. Sometimes Michael came home from work
with a Victoria's Secret box containing something lacy, wrapped
in pink tissue paper, and we'd make love during Letterman.

Other times, he brought ingredients for chocolate martinis
and we'd go out dancing until midnight.

We were as close as two people could be, and just when I
thought life couldn't get any better, the most amazing thing happened. I found out I was pregnant.

How effortless it all seemed.

Looking back, I sometimes wonder if it was all a dream. I suppose it was, because eventually I did wake from it. In fact, I sat straight up in bed, gasping my lungs out.

But let's not talk about that yet. There are still a few miracles to explore.

So let's talk about the baby.

CHAPTER

Four

He ere's the thing about motherhood. It exhausts you and thrills you. It kicks you in the butt, and the very next second makes you feel like a superstar. Most of all, it teaches you to be selfless.

Let me rephrase that. It doesn't really teach you this. It creates a new selflessness within you, which grabs hold of your heart when you first take your child into your arms. In that profound moment of extraordinary love and discovery, your own needs and desires become secondary. Nothing is as important as the well-being of your beautiful child. You would sacrifice anything for her. Even your own life. You would do it in a heartbeat. God wouldn't need to ask twice.

Our beautiful baby Megan was born on July 17, 2000. It was a difficult labor that lasted nineteen hours before ending in an emergency C-section, but I wouldn't change a single second of it. If that's what was required to bring Megan into the world, I would have done it ten times over.

For the next five days, while recovering from my surgery, I spent countless hours in the hospital holding her in my arms, fascinated by her movements and expressions. Her sweet, chubby face and tiny pink feet enchanted me. I was infatuated beyond comprehension by her soft black hair and puffy eyes, her sweet knees and plump belly, and her miniature little fingertips and nails. She was the most exquisite creature I had ever beheld, and my heart swelled with inexpressible love every time she squeaked or flexed her hands.

How clearly I remember lying on my side next to her in the hospital bed with my cheek resting on a hand, believing that I could lie there forever and never grow bored watching her. There was such truth in the simplicity of those moments.

Michael, too, was captivated by our new daughter. He went to work during the days, but spent the nights with us in our private room, sleeping in the upholstered chair.

When we finally brought Megan home, I came to realize that Michael was not only the perfect husband, but the perfect father as well.

He was nothing like my own father, who had always maintained an emotional distance. No...Michael changed diapers and couldn't seem to get enough of our baby girl. He carried Megan around the house in his arms. He read books to her and sang songs. A few times a week, he took her for long walks in the park so I could nap or have some time to myself, simply to shower or cook a meal. I felt like the luckiest woman alive.

Later, when Megan was out of diapers and had finally given up drinking from a bottle at the age of two, I began to feel that I was ready to start writing again.

Michael – always so generous and supportive – suggested that he take Megan to Connecticut every Sunday afternoon to visit his sister, Margery.

It worked out well. Margery was thrilled to spend time with them, and those happy day trips out of the city created an even stronger bond between Michael and Megan.

It wasn't long before I was submitting feature stories to a number of national parenting magazines. Always, in the back of my mind, however, was the dream of returning to the New Yorker, perhaps when Megan was older.

Sometimes I wonder if I would have done anything differently in those blissful days of new motherhood if I had known about the bomb that was about to drop onto our world. I believe I will always wonder that, and there will be no escaping the regrets, rational or otherwise.

When Megan was three-and-a-half years old, my father came to visit us in New York. It was the first time he had seen our house (we lived in a brownstone in Washington Square), and he mentioned repeatedly that he was sorry for not coming sooner. He said he was a "terrible grandfather."

"Don't worry about it, Dad," I replied as I passed the salad bowl across the table. "I've been terrible about visiting you, too. Life just gets so busy sometimes. I understand. It's hard to get away."

It was a lie, casually spoken, and we both knew it. Nothing had ever been easy between the two of us. There was an awkward tension that was obvious to everyone, including Michael, who was the one person in my life Dad actually approved of.

"You caught yourself a good man there," he gruffly said on our wedding day, then he patted Michael on the back and left early.

But of course he would love Michael. *Everyone* loved Michael. He was a handsome, charming, witty, Harvard-educated lawyer. A good provider and a devoted husband. As far as my father was concerned, Michael's small-town upbringing on a farm in the Midwest was the icing on the cake. I think Dad was still in shock that I had managed to marry such an amazing man.

We finished dinner and dessert, then Dad went off to bed at nine, not long after Megan fell asleep.

He planned to stay only twenty-four hours.

The following day, I worked hard to keep him busy and avoid any awkward silences or conversations about the past. Mom especially. It was not something we ever talked about.

Megan and I took him to the top of the Empire State Building, then we visited the Museum of Natural History, and of course, Ground Zero.

As he drove away, waving out the open car window, Megan slipped her tiny hand into mine, looked up at me with those big brown eyes and asked, "Will Grampy come back again?"

I hesitated a moment, then wet my lips and smiled. "Of course, sweetie, but he's very busy. I'm not sure when that will be."

We went back inside.

Michael was at work. The house seemed so empty and quiet.

"Want to make some cookies?" I cheerfully asked.

Megan gave me a melancholy look that will stay with me forever, because it was the first sign of the terrible nightmare that was about to befall our family.

I didn't know that then, of course. At the time, I didn't know *anything*.

"Okay," she replied.

I picked her up and carried her into the kitchen.

The following morning, Megan didn't wake until 8:30, which surprised me, because she was usually climbing onto our bed at six a.m. sharp. She was more dependable than our digital alarm clock.

When eight o'clock rolled around and she was still sleeping, I assumed she was tired from our sightseeing trip the day before.

I was wrong about that. It was something else entirely – something I never imagined would ever happen to us.

That was our last day of normal.

CHAPTER

Six

Over the next seven days, Megan grew increasingly lethargic and took long naps in the afternoons. Her skin was pale and she slumped in front of the television without ever smiling – not even for Captain Feathersword.

By week's end, she was irritable and couldn't bear it when I touched her, so I made an appointment with our doctor, who told me to bring her in right away.

As I was dressing Megan for the appointment, I noticed a large bruise on her left calf and another on her back. I mentioned this to the doctor, who sent us to the hospital for blood work.

Everything happened very quickly after that. The results came back an hour later, and Michael and I were called into the pediatrician's office for the results.

"I'm so sorry to have to tell you this," Dr. Jenkins said, "but Megan is very sick. The tests have indicated that she has acute myeloid leukemia."

She paused to give Michael and me a moment to absorb what she had told us, but I couldn't seem to process it. My brain wasn't working. Then suddenly I feared I might vomit. I wanted to tell the doctor that she was mistaken, but I knew it wasn't true. Something was very wrong with Megan, and I had known it before the blood work even came back.

"Are you all right, Mrs. Whitman?" the doctor asked.

Michael squeezed my hand.

I turned in my chair and looked out the open door at my sweet darling angel, who was lying quietly on the vinyl seats in the waiting area with a social worker. She was watching television and twirling her long brown hair around a finger.

I glanced briefly at Michael, who was white as a sheet, then faced the doctor again.

"I'd like to admit her through oncology for more tests," Dr. Jenkins said, "and start treatment right away."

No. It wasn't true. It wasn't happening. Not to Megan.

"Mrs. Whitman, are you all right?" Dr. Jenkins leaned forward over her desk.

"I'm fine," I said, though I was nothing of the sort. There was a crushing dread squeezing my chest as I imagined what was going to happen to Megan in the coming months. I knew enough about cancer to know that the treatment would not be easy. It was going to get much worse before it got better.

She was just a child. How was she ever going to cope with this? How was I going to cope?

"You say you want to begin treatment right away," Michael said, speaking up at last. "What if we don't agree? What if we want to get a second opinion?"

I glanced quickly at him, surprised at the note of accusation I heard in his voice.

"You're welcome to get a second opinion," Dr. Jenkins calmly replied, "but I strongly recommend that you allow us to admit Megan today. You shouldn't wait."

Michael stood up and began to pace around the office. He looked like he wanted to hit something.

"Is it that bad?" I asked. "Is there no time?"

There was an underlying note of confidence in the doctor's eyes, which provided me with a small measure of comfort. "Of course there's time," she said. "But it's important that we begin treatment immediately. It's also important that you try to stay positive. You're going to have a difficult battle ahead of you, but don't lose hope. The cure rate for leukemia in children is better than seventy-five percent. As soon as we get her admitted, we'll prepare the very best treatment plan possible. She's a strong girl. We're going to do everything we can to get her into remission."

My voice shook uncontrollably as I spoke. "Thank you."

I stood and walked out of the office in a daze, leaving Michael behind to talk to the doctor. I wondered how in the world I was ever going to explain any of this to Megan.

CHAPTER

Seven

There is nothing anyone can say or do which will ease your shock as a parent when you learn that your child has cancer. Your greatest wish – your deepest, intrinsic need – is to protect your child from harm. A disease like leukemia robs you of that power. There is no way to stop it from happening once it begins, and all you can do is place your trust in the doctors and nurses who are working hard to save your child's life. You feel helpless, afraid, grief-stricken, and angry. Some days you think it can't be real. It feels like a bad dream. You wish it was, but you can never seem to wake from it.

The first few days in the hospital were an endless array of X-rays, blood draws, intravenous lines, and lastly, a painful spinal tap to look for leukemia cells in the cerebrospinal fluid.

Not only did Michael and I have to get our heads around all of those tests and procedures, we had to educate ourselves about bone marrow aspirations, chemotherapy and all the side effects, as well as radiation treatments and stem cell transplants. In addition, we had to notify our friends and family. Everyone was supportive and came to our aid in some way – everyone except for my father, who remained distant as always.

He sent a get well card. That was all.

I pushed thoughts of him from my mind, however, because I had to stay strong for Megan.

I promised myself I would never cry in front of her. Instead, I cried every time I took a shower at the hospital (I never left), or I cried when Michael arrived and sent me downstairs to get something to eat. During those brief excursions outside the oncology ward, I would take a few minutes in a washroom somewhere and sob my heart out before venturing down to the cafeteria to force something into my stomach.

It was important to eat, I was told. The nurses reminded me on a daily basis that I had to stay healthy for Megan because she would be very susceptible to infection during treatment, and a fever could be fatal.

So I ate.

Every day, I ate.

Michael had a difficult time dealing with Megan's illness. Perhaps it had something to do with the loss of his brother when he was twelve. Some days he wouldn't come to the hospital until very late, and a few times I smelled whisky on his breath.

One night we argued about what we should say to Megan. He didn't want me to tell her that the chemo drugs would make her throw up.

I insisted that we had to always be honest with her. She needed to know that she could trust us to tell her the truth and be with her no matter how bad it got.

We never did agree on that, but I told her the truth anyway. Michael didn't speak to me for the next twenty-four hours.

"I don't want my hair to fall out," Megan said to me one afternoon, while we were waiting for the nurse to inject her with a combination of cytarabine, daunomycin, and etoposide. "I want to go home."

I dug deep for the strength to keep my voice steady. "I know it's going to be hard, sweetie," I replied, "but we don't have a choice about this. If you don't have the treatment, you won't get better, and we need you to get better. I promise I'll be right here with you the entire time, right beside you, loving you. You're a brave girl and we're going to get through this. We'll get through it together. You and me."

She kissed me on the cheek and said, "Okay, Mommy."

I held her as close as I could, kissed the top of her head, and prayed that the treatment would not be too painful.

Megan's hair did fall out, and she was extremely ill from the chemotherapy, but within four weeks, she achieved complete remission.

I'll never forget the day when those test results came back.

Rain was coming down in buckets outside, and the sky was the color of ash.

I was standing in front of the window in the hospital playroom, staring out at the water pelting the glass, while Megan played alone at a table with her doll. I told myself that no matter what happened, we would get through it.

We would not stop fighting.

We would conquer this.

Then Dr. Jenkins walked into the room with a clipboard under her arm and smiled at me. I knew from the look in her eye that it was good news, and my relief was so overwhelming, I could not speak or breathe.

A sob escaped me. I dropped to my knees and wept violently into my hands.

This was the first time Megan saw me cry. She set down her doll and came over to rub my back with her tiny, gentle hand.

"Don't cry, Mommy," she said. "Everything's going to be okay. You'll see."

I laughed as I looked up at her, and pulled her into my loving arms.

After a short period of recuperation, Megan entered a phase of post-remission therapy, which consisted of more chemo drugs to ensure that any residual cancer cells would not multiply and return.

I wish I could say that our lives returned to normal, but after facing the very real possibility of our daughter's death, I knew the old "normal" would never exist for us again. Our lives were changed forever, and some of those changes were extraordinary.

From that day forward, I saw more beauty in the world than I had ever seen before. I cherished every moment, found joy in the tiniest pleasures, for I understood this amazing gift called *life*.

I gloried in the time we spent together, knowing how precious and fragile it all was. Sometimes I would look up at the sky and watch the clouds shift and roll across the vibrant expanse of blue, and I wanted to weep from its sheer majesty.

We lived in a beautiful world, and I felt so fortunate to have Megan at my side. I had learned that I was stronger than I ever imagined I was, and so was Megan. She had fought a difficult battle and had become my hero. I respected and admired her – more than I ever respected or admired anyone. I was in awe of her.

In addition, friends and family offered us help and support, and I saw, through the eyes of my heart, how incredibly lucky we all were to be on the receiving end of all that generosity and compassion. It was something wonderful to witness, and I felt truly blessed.

It may seem an odd thing to say, but I sometimes felt that Megan's cancer, even though it was painful, had brought something good. It had taught us so much about life and love. I had grown – so had she – and I knew that this change in us was very profound and would affect both our futures.

Later I would learn how right I was.

For something both glorious and mystifying still awaited us.

O ver the next two years, I helped Megan through her post-remission therapy and cherished every precious moment with her, basking in the joy of our existence.

Michael reacted differently.

He was overjoyed, of course, when Megan achieved remission. We celebrated and went to Disney World for the weekend. But slowly, over time, as the weeks pressed on and there was still no end to the doctor appointments and pills and blood work, he began to withdraw.

Every evening when he came home from work, he poured himself a drink. Though he never consumed enough to become noticeably intoxicated, it was enough to change the core of the person he had once been.

He smiled less often (oh, how I missed his smile) and he left all of Megan's medical care to me. He didn't attend any of her appointments, nor did he stay informed about her medications at home. I administered all of them myself.

The Sunday trips to his sister's house in Connecticut fell by the wayside as well, along with my writing.

Not that I cared about that. Being with Megan was all that mattered to me – but perhaps that was part of the problem where Michael was concerned.

In the early days of our marriage, when we were passionately in love, he was the center of my world. Maybe he couldn't accept the fact that I had a *new* hero now, and there were things in life I revered more than his success at the firm or our expensive dinners out.

These were things he didn't understand.

"They're just clouds," he would say when I wanted to lay on the grass and watch them roll across the sky. He would frown at me as I shook out the blanket. "Don't be so emotional. It's ridiculous."

Or maybe *that* was the heart of the problem. Maybe he couldn't handle the complexity of his own emotions. We had come very close to losing our daughter, and sometimes it felt like we were still standing on a thin sheet of ice with a deep crack down its center.

What if it happened again? What if Megan relapsed? What if we had another child and the same thing happened? How would we cope?

It had been so difficult the first time. I couldn't imagine going through anything like that again.

I understood his fear. I felt it, too, but it didn't keep me from loving Megan or spending time with her. It only intensified our bond.

I wanted to be closer to Michael, but he was always too tired, not in the mood, or too busy.

Once, I suggested that we try therapy together – surely a child with cancer was enough to warrant a few sessions with a professional – but he was worried that someone at the firm might find out, and he was determined to stay strong. He was a partner now and couldn't afford to be weak.

His behavior saddened and angered me, and I regret to say that this wedge in our relationship only grew deeper over time. I felt more and more disconnected from the love we once shared.

Consequently, when the next bomb hit, our foundations were unsteady. As a couple, we were damaged and vulnerable, and it all went downhill from there.

On a snowy late November afternoon in 2005, I was putting away the dishes, and Megan screamed in the bathroom. As soon as I heard the terror in her voice, I dropped a plate on the floor. It shattered into a hundred pieces on the ceramic tiles, and my heart dropped to my stomach.

Please, let it be a spider, I thought as I ran to her.

When I pushed the door open, I found her sitting on the floor with blood pouring out of her nose. She was slumped over, trying to catch it in her hands.

Quickly I grabbed a towel, held it under her nose and helped her up. "It's all right, honey. Mommy's here now. Everything's going to be fine."

But I knew it was not that simple. She was not fine. She'd been fatigued for the past week and had lost her appetite.

I don't know how I managed to think clearly as I helped her out to the front hall. All I wanted to do was cry or yell at someone, but I could do none of those things because I had to focus on picking up my purse, locking the door behind me, buckling her into the car, and driving to the hospital.

After two years in remission with normal blood counts and an excellent prognosis, Megan suffered a relapse in her central nervous system.

The doctor explained that this type of relapse occurred in less than ten percent of childhood leukemia patients, and that Megan would require frequent spinal taps to inject chemotherapy drugs directly into her cerebrospinal fluid.

I tried to call Michael on his cell phone, but he wasn't answering and the receptionist couldn't tell me where he was.

I was enraged. I remember thinking, as I stood at the nurses' station and slammed the receiver down, that I wanted to divorce him. Why wasn't he here with me? Why did I have to shoulder all of this alone? Did he not care? Didn't he love his daughter? Didn't he love *me*?

I sat down on a bench in the hospital corridor and struggled to calm myself before I returned to Megan's bedside, but my heart was throbbing in my chest and I was afraid I might, at any second, start screaming like a lunatic.

Why was this happening? Recently, I had begun to feel some security that Megan was going to be all right and live a long, happy life. She would go to high school, college, get married and have children of her own. I was certain that one day, all of this would be a distant memory, because we had fought hard and beaten it.

But the cancer was back. The treatments had not worked. The leukemia cells were infecting her blood again.

I stood up and ran to the nearest bathroom, where I heaved up the entire contents of my stomach.

⟶

Sometime after eleven that night, Michael arrived at the hospital. I had no idea where he'd been all day or why he hadn't answered his phone. I didn't ask. All I did was explain Megan's diagnosis in a calm and cool manner, because by that time, I had reached a state of numbness. Megan was sleeping and I couldn't seem to feel anything. I couldn't cry, couldn't yell. I couldn't even step into Michael's arms to let him hold me.

I suppose I had been enduring this alone for such a long time that I didn't need him anymore. I didn't need anyone – except for Megan, and the doctors and nurses who could keep her alive.

When Michael absorbed what I told him about the nosebleed and the fatigue over the past week, and the spinal taps and radiation she would require, he pushed me aside, marched up to the nurses' station, and smacked his palm down upon the countertop.

A nurse was seated in front of a computer, talking to someone on the phone. "I'll get right back to you," she said, then set the receiver down and looked up at him. "Is there something I can do for you, sir?"

"Where the hell is Dr. Jenkins?" Michael asked. "Get her out here. *Now.* She has a lot to answer for."

I rushed forward and grabbed hold of his arm. "It's not her fault, Michael. She's doing everything she can for Megan."

He roughly shook me away. "Everything? What kind of hospital is this? Why didn't anyone see this coming?"

"Keep your voice down," I said. "You'll wake Megan. She'll hear you."

A baby started to cry somewhere down the hall.

"I don't care if she hears me! She needs to know that at least *someone* is looking out for her."

My stomach muscles clenched tight. I could feel my blood rushing to my head, pounding in my ears.

"*Someone?*" I replied. "Like who? *You?* Pardon me for saying so, Michael, but you've done nothing for Megan over the past two years. I've taken care of her every minute of every day, while you find other more important things to do. So don't you *dare* pretend to be her savior tonight. I won't let you make enemies out of the very people who are trying to save her."

I gestured toward the nurse – though I didn't even know her name – and she slowly stood up.

She was a tall, broad-shouldered black woman with plastic-rimmed glasses and a fierce-looking gaze. "Is there going to be a problem here, sir?" she asked. "Do I need to call security?"

Briefly he considered it, then turned his back on her and faced me. A muscle twitched at his jaw as he spoke. "I told you we should've gotten a second opinion."

Michael reached into his breast pocket, pulled out a business card, and tossed it onto the counter. He pointed a threatening finger at the nurse. "See that? Yeah. You're going to hear from me."

He walked out and left me standing there with my heart racing, perspiration beading upon my forehead.

Not because I was afraid, but because it had taken every ounce of self-control I possessed not to punch Michael in the face.

I took a few deep breaths to calm myself.

"Was that your ex?" the nurse asked.

I glanced at her nametag. "No…Jean. We're still married."

Jean removed her glasses, pulled a tissue from the box on the counter, and proceeded to clean her lenses while she strolled out from behind the counter.

She approached me, slid her glasses back on, then laid a hand on my shoulder. "You look like you could use a Popsicle."

Not knowing what else to say, I simply nodded and followed her into the lunchroom.

CHAPTER

Eleven

❧

Early the next morning, Michael stepped off the elevator and found me reading a magazine in the lounge area outside Megan's room. He explained that he'd had a few too many drinks at dinner the night before with an important client, and that the shock of Megan's relapse had been too much for him. He apologized for his behavior.

Raking a hand through his hair, pacing back and forth, he admitted that he just needed to blame someone. He felt guilty for all of his absences over the past two years. Then he stopped pacing, looked me straight in the eye, and promised to try harder to be there for us in the coming months.

I closed the distance between us and clasped both his hands in mine. Tears filled my eyes as I remembered how, at the age of twelve, he had dealt with a similar family tragedy when he lost his brother.

"It's okay," I gently said. "This has been rough on both of us. We just have to stick together, that's all. We have to be a team."

He pulled me into his arms and held me for a long, long time.

When I finally stepped back, I said, "Can I make a suggestion?"

He nodded.

"It would help if you could spend some time with Megan this morning. She misses you, and she's scheduled for a radiation treatment this afternoon. It would lift her spirits."

Michael's shoulders rose and fell as he took a deep breath and let it out. "Sure. Okay. Why don't you go get yourself a cup of coffee or something. Looks like you could use a break. You've been doing so much. You've been amazing. You know that, right?"

A lump the size of an orange formed in my throat. It was the first time my husband had ever acknowledged my unyielding devotion to our daughter. "Thank you."

I started down the corridor, but he called out to me. "Sophie, wait."

I stopped and turned, waited for him to approach.

"Do you ever think about having another baby?" he asked as he stood before me at the elevator.

I hesitated. "Um, not really. I certainly wouldn't want to try to get pregnant *now*."

"Why not?" he asked. "I know things aren't perfect, but maybe another child could give us something to feel hopeful about."

My gut turned over, and I felt a little queasy. "I *do* feel hopeful. Every day I cling to that hope. Megan feels hopeful, too, but it's not just that. If I got pregnant, she might think we're trying to replace her." I paused. "No, Michael. Not now. It's not a good time."

His gaze darted back down the hall. "You're probably right. I'm sorry. I shouldn't have brought it up. Maybe when she's feeling better, we can talk about it then."

I touched his arm. "We will, Michael. I promise. You just caught me off guard, that's all."

I pushed the elevator button and watched him walk away, then rode the three floors down to the cafeteria, where I sat alone, sipping my hot coffee in silence, watching people come and go.

I thought of what Michael had said and felt numb all over again, as if I were nothing but a cold, lifeless mass of human matter. I couldn't move, nor did I wish to make eye contact with anyone who might suddenly strike up a friendly conversation. Lord help me if I had to explain myself…

No, I'm not here to visit someone…My five-year-old daughter is ill, and I'll be sleeping here every night for the indefinite future until she's well enough to go home.

And my husband wants me to get pregnant.

I shuddered.

Why did he want that?

In case Megan died?

After about twenty minutes, my cell phone rang. The call display said "Michael," and a fireball of anxiety exploded in my belly. Was something wrong? Did Megan need me?

With clumsy, fumbling hands, I flipped the phone open. "Hi, is everything okay? You're not supposed to use your cell phone in the hospital."

"Yeah, everything's fine," he replied. "But I can't stay much longer. I need to get back to the office. There's an important court date coming up. Are you finished your coffee yet?"

I pinched the bridge of my nose and felt my stomach churn with acid. "Yeah, I'm done. I'll be right there."

"Great."

I stood and gathered up my purse. "Just stay with her for a few more minutes, okay? Please don't leave until I'm back on the floor."

"Sure," he replied. "See you in five." *Click.*

Just like that, the connection went dead.

Over the next three weeks, Megan was treated with aggressive chemotherapy and craniospinal radiation, while we prepared ourselves for an allogeneic bone marrow transplant, which the doctor said was her best option.

Her hair fell out again, and she was violently ill most days.

On one particular afternoon (although it might have been the morning; it was all such a blur at that point) I had to fight hard not to fall apart completely when the nurses came in to weigh Megan. She was too weak to get up, so they weighed me instead, then instructed me to pick her up and hold her as I stepped back onto the scale.

She wore nothing but her pink princess underwear and yellow SpongeBob socks, and she was completely bald with a jungle of tubes sticking out of her in every direction. I had to be careful not to become tangled in them.

While the nurse recorded our combined weight, Megan rested her head on my shoulder. When they were finished, I gently laid her back down on the bed and climbed in next to her. For a long time, I stroked her smooth, warm head while she slept.

"I'm sorry, Mommy," she said, opening her eyes at last.

She touched my cheek, wiped my tears away, and told me not to worry. She promised that everything was going to be okay.

Unfortunately, neither Michael nor I was a stem cell match for Megan, so we had to rely on the National Marrow Donor Program to find an unrelated donor.

Dr. Jenkins told us not to beat ourselves up about it because according to the most recent statistics, parents match up with their children less than one percent of the time, while only twenty-five percent of siblings are complete matches.

This helped to alleviate some of my guilt over not having had a second child who might have been a perfect match and could have saved Megan's life.

This was our reality, and we had to work around it as best we could.

Thankfully, by some miracle, a donor was found quickly, which was a blessing, even though Dr. Jenkins informed us that the risk of complications increased if the donor was not a full match, which he (or she) was not. But it was our only hope.

I was relieved when Michael was able to leave the office to be present during the procedure. We both sat on opposite sides of Megan's bed while Nurse Jean brought in the harvested marrow to be injected into Megan's bloodstream.

It was a simple IV bag filled with blood, which was hooked up to Megan's central venous catheter.

We were quite concerned over the fact that she was still very weak from a recent high dose of chemo drugs, which was necessary to kill off the remaining cancer cells in her body and make room for the new, healthy stem cells. But Dr. Jenkins assured us that the transplant would help make her stronger, so we soldiered on.

I was fascinated and filled with hope as I watched the blood flow through the clear rubber tubing into my daughter's body.

The procedure itself was over in no time at all – it lasted about 45 minutes – which hardly seemed possible.

Even more surprising was that another hour later, Megan's color began to improve, and she began to laugh at SpongeBob on the television. I couldn't believe it. How quickly it had infused life back into her veins!

The nurses told us that it happened that way sometimes, but I just thought Megan was special, and that some higher power was looking out for us.

Even so, it was still going to be a long recovery, we were told, and I knew what lay ahead of us. We would need to spend weeks or perhaps months in the hospital and continue with her therapy, but I was prepared for anything. I would have given up my own life to save her.

Later, while Megan continued to giggle at the shenanigans on her favorite cartoon, Michael stood up, came around the bed, and began to massage my shoulders. He kissed the top of my head, and I pulled his hand to my cheek, pressed my lips to the warmth of his palm.

Perhaps everything was going to be okay after all, I told myself. Maybe there was hope that we could be a normal family again. Maybe we would even have more children.

We laughed and talked and forgave each other for everything.

That night, I cried again in the shower, but this time they were tears of joy. I laughed in relief as I wiped them away, and later, while my hair was still wet, Michael and I made love in the back seat of his car in the farthest corner of the hospital garage.

It had been a good day, and I treasured it.

CHAPTER

Fourteen

Six weeks later, Megan developed interstitial pneumonitis, a serious pneumonia that is associated with graft-versus-host disease.

I had known that GVHD was a potential complication of the transplant, for Megan's immunity had been greatly diminished by her chemotherapy beforehand. I was also told that under normal circumstances, it would take six to twelve months to recover immunity, but now, because of the GVHD, it could take years.

I fought to stay positive, while Michael threatened a lawsuit.

"*Please*, Michael." I begged him over and over not to burden Dr. Jenkins with court dates and legal problems. "We knew the risks of the transplant and we chose to go ahead with it anyway. Besides, we have enough of a battle as it is, just helping Megan stay strong. She needs to believe that we're all on the same team."

But he wouldn't stop laying blame. Nor would he talk to Dr. Jenkins about anything. He refused to be in the same room with her, which meant he stayed away from the hospital whenever she was on duty.

Things only got worse after that. Megan developed veno-occlusive disease, another complication of the transplant, which was affecting her liver. It explained her constant fever, the painful diarrhea, and the strange rash that had broken out all over her small, frail body.

The medical team ordered platelet transfusions, diuretics, and anti-clotting medications.

When the pain in her belly escalated sharply one evening, I called Michael right away and told him to come to the hospital, even though Dr. Jenkins was in charge of Megan's care.

He said he would be there soon, in twenty minutes.

Two hours later, he stepped off the elevator – but it was too late.

He had waited too long.

Fifteen

ᶜᶜᔆᔆᵔᵔ

February 19, 2006

Despite the heroic efforts of the doctors and nurses who did everything they could to save her, Megan passed away ten minutes before Michael arrived.

The death of my child was the death of my own heart. That night in the hospital was pure agony. I cried for hours and refused to leave her. Finally, they had to escort me out of her room so they could take her body to the morgue.

The funeral, four days later, was a deep black hole of sorrow and disbelief. I was flooded with despair. I ached over the decision to go ahead with the bone marrow transplant.

Perhaps if we had waited, we might have found a better match, or perhaps her life would have been prolonged, even for a year or two.

I felt no peace.

All I wanted was to hold her in my arms again, to breathe in the sweet scent of her skin, press my lips to the top of her head.

I couldn't believe she was gone, that I would never see her again, never hold her, never hear the sound of her laughter. I wanted to climb into the coffin with her and go wherever it was that she had gone.

I didn't know where that was, and it *killed* me. It killed me not to know where my child was, or whether or not she was safe.

Who was taking care of her? Was she scared?

I cannot say anything more than that.

There are simply no words. It is inexpressible.

Ⓜy sister Jen was a great comfort to me when Megan died. She came immediately and helped with the funeral arrangements, and took a leave of absence from work to stay with us for a month.

She held me when I cried, and talked to me of other things when I needed a distraction from the crushing weight of my grief.

Some days were especially difficult, but Jen always had the wisdom to say the right thing, and more importantly, she knew what not to say, because she, like me, understood loss. We were both very young when we said goodbye to our mother.

Michael, however, who also understood loss, seemed somehow immune to the intensity of grief I was experiencing. I never saw him cry, and he usually left the room whenever I fell apart, which happened quite often that first month.

Thank God for Jen. I never would have gotten through any of it without her.

I received many sympathy cards from friends and family, and they were all deeply appreciated during that very dark time. One, especially, touched my heart.

It arrived late, two months after Megan's death, and it came from Kirk Duncan, my old boyfriend from high school. It had been more than ten years since we last communicated by email, so I was surprised when I saw the return address on the envelope.

Dear Sophie,

I am terribly sorry to hear about the loss of your daughter. I can't imagine the pain you are going through, but please know that you and your husband are in my thoughts.

I took the liberty of making a donation to the oncology department in the children's hospital in my area, which I put in your family's name. I wish there was more I could do, but I hope this small gesture will let you know that I am thinking of you and your family.

Your friend, Kirk

I cried when I first read it, then reread it a number of times that day.

How grateful I was for this thoughtful act from such an old and beloved friend.

That night I slipped the card into the pages of a hardcover picture book that I had kept from my childhood. It was a book my mother used to read to me – one of the few things I had left of her; the rest of the memories had been packed away and stored in the past.

After Jen left, I discovered how generous and compassionate some people could be. One neighbor in particular, an older lady named Lois who lived on my street, came by every few days, always with a plate of something to eat, which was a blessing, for I had very little appetite and no interest in cooking. Sometimes she brought a casserole that I could heat up for dinner. Other times she brought homemade cookies, still warm from her oven.

She sat with me at my kitchen table in the afternoons and talked to me about everything from the weather to the death of her husband ten years before. She was an excellent listener. Whenever I spoke about Megan, she nodded caringly and agreed that she was a beautiful, extraordinary child.

Lois was very kind, and if not for the expectation of her afternoon visits, I probably wouldn't have gotten dressed most days.

She was lovely to me, and I will always cherish her friendship during that difficult first year. Not only did she help me with my grief over Megan, she was there to help me deal with the uncomfortable issues in my crumbling marriage.

C H A P T E R

Seventeen

ᴄᴄ◦◦

Six months after the funeral, I came home from the food market one day to find Michael's BMW parked out front, which was an odd occurrence, since he never came home in the afternoons.

I juggled my grocery bags as I unlocked the front door, and glanced curiously into the living room, then peered into the dining room as well.

The house was quiet. It didn't appear that anyone was home.

I went to the kitchen, set the bags down on the counter, and called out to him. "Michael, are you home?"

Still, no reply.

I wondered if he had gone out to the backyard. I stepped onto the deck, but there was no sign of him anywhere, so I went back inside. "Michael?"

Quickly, I climbed the stairs, thinking he might have come home sick, or perhaps something terrible had happened.

My heart began to pound as I put one foot in front of the other, and a heavy knot of dread tightened in my belly. This was not unusual. I'd been experiencing bouts of anxiety since Megan's death, always fearing the worst in any situation...

When I reached the top of the stairs, I found our bedroom empty, but Megan's door wide open, which was *definitely* unusual, for Michael insisted we keep it closed.

He didn't want to go in there. He didn't want to look at Megan's things, or smell the familiar scent of her that still lingered. He didn't want to be reminded.

A part of me understood this on some level, but another part of me did not. Sometimes when I missed Megan, and the longing became unbearable, I would go to her room and sit on her bed. I would leaf through her books, run a hand over her stuffed animals. Then I might lie down for a while and imagine her lying beside me.

I felt her presence all around me. She would place her tiny, warm hand on my cheek, as she had done so many times in our life together, and tell me that everything was going to be okay. "I'm better now, Mommy," she would say. I took great comfort from those daydreams.

Michael didn't understand it at all. He believed I was only making it harder on myself. He told me that she was gone, and we had to put it behind us. We had to focus on the future.

Perhaps that's why I was so unnerved by the sight of her open door. Would I find my unshakable husband lying on the bed as I so often did? Would I find him weeping?

I braced myself as I made my way down the narrow hall.

Michael turned and looked at me with hostility as I entered. "I thought I told you to keep this door shut."

I was baffled by his anger. It wasn't what I had expected.

"I'm sorry, I must have forgotten. What are you doing home so early?"

"I had to change my tie," he said. "I spilled something on it at lunch." He shut Megan's closet door and moved to the center of the room.

Placing his hands on his hips, he gazed all around at the evidence of her life – the white dresser with her jewelry box on top, the bunny posters on the wall, and the basket piled high with stuffed animals.

"We need to clean this room out." He wouldn't look at me. "We can give all her toys and clothes away to the Salvation Army. She would have wanted that. She was always generous."

I swallowed uneasily and took a few steps closer. "Yes, she was, but I'm not ready for that yet. I like to come in here sometimes. It makes me feel close to her."

He gave me that look – the one that made me feel foolish and weak. "She's gone, Sophie. You're going to have to accept that sooner or later."

A flash of anger sparked within me. "It's only been six months."

"Yes. Six excruciating months. You do nothing but sit around and cry, and this room is like a tomb. It's depressing to come home at night. I think it would be best if we had someone come over and collect her things. The furniture too." He took a step closer and spoke in a gentler, more encouraging tone. "We could get you a new desk and a computer. Turn this into an office. You should go back to your writing."

I frowned. "I can't *write*. Not now. I need time to grieve."

"But you can't just wallow in it, Sophie. What you need to do is try harder to get over it. We both need to get on with our lives."

I shook my head. "No! Maybe you're ready to move on, but I'm not. I'm still in agony. I can't just forget about her, or pretend she never existed."

"That's not what I'm saying."

"Then what are you saying, exactly?"

He turned his gaze to the window. For a long moment, neither of us spoke.

"Just forget it," he said as he brushed by me, heading for the door. "I need to get back to work. I'll probably be late getting home. Why don't you get a movie for yourself."

As I watched him leave, the floor seemed to shift under my feet. I felt like I was standing in a teetering rowboat, struggling to keep my balance while the waves splashed against my hull.

My father called that night. It was the first time he had called since the funeral.

His lifelong remoteness hit me particularly hard after my argument with Michael. I began to feel as if I would always be disappointed by the men in my life. My husband didn't seem to understand a single thing I was feeling, and quite frankly, I didn't understand him either. How could he be ready to move on? Had he not loved Megan as much as I did? Or was he burying himself in denial? *If you push it away, it won't hurt you.* Is that what he thought?

"Hi Dad," I said, as I sat down at the kitchen table and cupped my forehead in a hand. "How are you?"

And what do you want? What could you possibly say to me now, after a lifetime of disapproval and indifference? I suppose, like Michael, you're going to tell me to stop crying and get over it.

"I'm fine," he replied. "How are things with you?"

Great. Just what I needed. Light conversation.

I checked my watch and wondered how long this would take.

"I've been better." My voice broke on the last word, however, and hot tears flooded my eyes. I slapped my hand over my mouth in a desperate attempt to crush the threat of a complete emotional breakdown. I couldn't do that in front of my father. Not him.

"Sounds like you're having a rough day."

I swallowed over the urge to let out a gut-wrenching sob. "Yeah."

I wiped at the tears, stood up, and filled the kettle at the sink while I clenched the phone between my shoulder and ear.

"We all loved Megan," he softly said. "She was a special girl. I'm so sorry, Sophie."

That was it. I couldn't hold it in any longer. I shut off the water, set the kettle down on the granite countertop and wept into the phone.

"Thank you, Daddy. That means a lot to me. I'm taking it pretty hard."

"Of course you are. She was your daughter."

I tried again to stop crying, but it was no use. The tears were gushing out of my eyes.

My father was quiet on the other end of the line, and when he finally spoke, his voice quavered. "It's never easy to lose someone you love."

Though he didn't say it, I knew he was talking about Mom. Nothing was ever the same after she left us that day back in 1984. I was fourteen years old, and I remember watching her go through security at the airport. I waved goodbye, but I *hated* her for leaving us. I hated her.

I hated her most for leaving me with Dad.

Oh, how I had willed her to come back. *If you love me, you won't leave us.* I shut my eyes and whispered out loud, "Turn around, don't go."

But she left anyway.

We moved two months later. Dad couldn't bear to go on living in the house that reminded us all of *her*...

He was a lot like Michael.

"I don't know how I'm going to get through this," I said to him on the telephone, as I wiped my nose with the back of my hand.

"You will," he replied. "You just need to take it slow, one day at a time. Don't rush yourself. It's okay to be sad. Just know that..." He paused, then began again. "I want you to know that I'm here for you. I wasn't always the best father. I didn't always make the right decisions, and I'm sorry for that, but if there's anything I can do, just say the word."

After I recovered from my astonishment, I thanked him and hung up the phone – and experienced a muted warmth that felt something like comfort.

Perhaps there was hope for happiness as well, some day in the future. Perhaps I wouldn't always feel so disappointed.

I set the kettle on the burner to boil and tore the plastic off a new box of tea.

CHAPTER

Eighteen

❧

A few days after our argument in Megan's bedroom, I cooked a special dinner for Michael. His favorite: maple-glazed salmon with garlic mashed potatoes, and fresh sautéed vegetables.

I showered and put on a skirt (he always told me I looked good in skirts), set the table with the fine china we received as a wedding gift, and set out some candles.

I wanted to explain to him that I needed time. That was all.

Our conversation in the hospital – the one about having another child – kept bouncing around in my brain. I wanted to ask him to be patient with me. I was not in a good place right now, but maybe one day I would feel ready for something more.

Just not now. Not yet.

He called at six and told me he would be home at seven, so I prepared everything, poured myself a glass of wine, lit the candles, and sat down at the table to wait.

He walked in the door at midnight.

I had already given up waiting, had put the food in plastic containers in the fridge, changed into my pajamas, and gone to bed to watch television.

I listened to him putter around in the kitchen downstairs. I heard the buttons on the microwave as he reheated the salmon. A short while later he shuffled heavily up the stairs.

I quickly shut off the TV and slid under the covers. I just couldn't face him. I didn't want to talk. I certainly didn't want to ask why he was so late, and risk getting into an argument.

He slipped into bed a few minutes later, and I pretended to be asleep.

CHAPTER

Nineteen

❧

Nine months after the death of our child, Michael came home from work, sat me down on the leather sofa in the living room, and told me he was leaving me.

He explained that he couldn't bear the tears anymore, that I wasn't the same woman he had married, and that he deserved a brighter future.

As I sat there staring at his impossibly handsome face – he only got better looking with age – my brain stopped working. I didn't burst into tears. I suppose I didn't have any tears left to shed.

I was speechless, however. Not that I was surprised. I wasn't. We had been soul mates once – madly, passionately in love – but all that seemed so far away now. It was another lifetime. I was thirty-six now, and so much had happened since those early days of dining out and making love on the living room carpet.

He was right. I was no longer the woman he married. I wasn't a rising star in the New York publishing world anymore. I didn't wear skirts and heels. Instead, I was an emotionally battered, grief-stricken, stay-at-home mother who wasn't even a mother anymore, because I'd just buried my daughter in the ground.

We both knew we were no longer connected. We didn't share the same feelings, and our ideas about the future were vastly different.

We were no longer in love.

"Maybe we just need a little more time," I dutifully suggested, making one last attempt to save our marriage, for I had never been a quitter, and quite frankly the notion of any more loss in my life made me want to throw up. "It's only been nine months."

He shook his head. "Things were off kilter before that, and you know it as well as I do. I don't think there's any way to fix this."

"But I don't want to just give up," I argued. "Do you really believe that you'd be happier on your own? We were a team once. Maybe we can be like that again."

He was sitting forward with his elbows on his knees. He gazed down at his hands, rubbed the pad of his thumb over his palm.

"I'm not going to be on my own," he explained. For a long time he was quiet, then at last he looked up and met my stricken eyes. "I'm in love with someone else, Sophie, and she's pregnant."

My vision blurred for a few seconds, and the whole world went white, then slowly came back into focus.

Sitting back against the leather seat cushions, I inhaled a deep breath and let it out, while I tried to comprehend the fact that there was nothing I could say or do to save my marriage. It was too late. It was dead. Michael was having a baby with someone else. He had moved on after Megan, while my heart was still cloaked in black.

So much for being a fighter. I had no more fight left in me. At least not when it came to holding onto my husband.

The divorce, however, was another matter entirely.

I sat forward, too, rested my elbows on my knees and looked him square in the eye. "You better not try to screw me over, Michael. If you do, I swear I'll wipe the floor with you."

He considered that for a moment, then stood up and nodded at me. "I don't doubt it. And I'm sorry, Sophie. I really am."

With nothing more to say, he walked out.

In the end, Michael proved himself to be very generous and highly accommodating in the divorce. Not only did he give me our house in Washington Square, but he also awarded me a large cash settlement, which I used to buy a new car (because he kept the BMW), as well as a monthly alimony check for as long as I remained unmarried.

I suppose he felt guilty for cheating on me while I was taking care of our dying daughter.

I didn't bother to appease him. I let him keep his guilt.

I was driving in my new car, running errands one bright sunny morning, when I saw them together – Michael and his lovely young fiancée, strolling along Seventh Avenue. They were holding hands and looking abominably happy.

Her name was Lucy Wright. She was a young associate at the law firm. She had bouncy blonde hair and wore a knee-length sundress with yellow splashes of brown-eyed Susans printed on the skirt, and high wedge sandals.

She was exceptionally attractive. There was no denying it. She had that certain spark. It was the same spark I once had myself, before the exhausting, debilitating collapse of my world. It's what attracted Michael to me in the first place.

As I drove past them, her round belly registered in my brain, and I was suddenly overcome by a firestorm of jealousy. Not because she had taken my husband from me and was now sharing his bed. It had nothing to do with Michael, and I knew in that moment that I was over him.

What I envied was her optimism. She was looking forward to all the joys of motherhood without any of the dread or fear that I would feel if I were in her place.

In that moment, I became conscious of the fact that I would never experience that blissful optimism again. I would not be courageous enough to have another child.

I wasn't even sure I would ever be brave enough to love someone —and that thought made me pull over onto the side of the road and sit in silence for a long, long time.

CHAPTER

Twenty

⋘✦⋙

February 12, 2007

As the first anniversary of Megan's death approached, I had a terrible nightmare. I was back in the ICU, and the doctors and nurses were rushing around her bed in a panic, shooting drugs into her IV tubes, performing CPR – all in a last minute, hopeless attempt to save her life.

Then suddenly her eyes flew open, she reached out to me and said, "Don't leave me, Mommy. I'm scared!"

My eyes flew open as well, and for the next hour, I lay in bed, tossing and turning, sinking deeper and deeper into a painful well of memories as I replayed those horrors in my mind. I knew I had to stop thinking about her death, stop worrying about where she was now – if she was anywhere at all – and focus instead on the joy she had brought to my life.

I forced myself to recall those special years during remission, when I began to see the world with new eyes. For a while, I had understood and cherished the extraordinary gift of my existence on this planet, and I relished each new day with my daughter.

I wondered what she would think if she could see me now, wallowing in my grief. Alone.

I imagined she would grieve for me in return.

That single thought prompted me to climb out of bed. I boiled an egg for breakfast, took a long shower, then called my sister and asked if I could come and visit for a few days. I wanted to talk about the possibility of going back to work. I had no interest in writing – at least not yet – but I thought I might be able to do some freelance editing.

"That sounds like a great idea," Jen said. "Joe and I were just talking about you yesterday. And Megan, of course. We miss you. Please come. How soon can you be here?"

"Just give me an hour to pack."

True to my word, exactly one hour later, I was buttoning up my sheepskin coat and tossing my suitcase into the back of my compact SUV.

As I drove out of the city on that mild winter day, I could feel Megan's presence in the back seat. Every so often, I glanced in the rearview mirror, and I could see her smiling at me.

The only time she spoke was to remind me to turn north onto the 684.

She stayed with me until I passed Hartford, then quietly departed and left me to find my own way to my sister's house in Manchester.

Not long after I crossed the border into New Hampshire, the temperature plummeted. If I had been out walking, I would have felt it on my cheeks. The chill would have entered my throat and lungs, but I was strapped tightly into the cozy confines of my vehicle with the heat blasting out of the dashboard vents, and was therefore shielded from the conditions outside.

I will always wonder what brought that deer out onto the road just as the puddles from the melting snow turned to ice. I saw her out of the corner of my eye, galloping onto the pavement, and my whole body went rigid.

Wrenching the steering wheel left to avoid her, I hit the brakes at the same time, which was, of course, the worst thing I could have done.

The car whipped around 180 degrees, so I was now facing the oncoming headlights from the vehicles traveling behind me. My tires skimmed sideways across the pavement toward the shoulder of the road.

I remember everything in excruciating detail, the noise especially, as my car rolled five times down the steep embankment. Glass shattered and smashed. Steel collapsed. The world spun in dizzying circles in front of my eyes, so I shut them and gripped the steering wheel hard, bracing my body against the jarring impact as the roof collapsed over the passenger side and the windows blew out.

Down I went, tumbling and bouncing over the rocks like a stone skipping across water.

Then all at once, it was over.

There was only white noise in my ears, and the thunderous sound of my heartbeat.

I opened my eyes to find myself hanging upside down in my seatbelt, with the side of my head wedged up against the roof.

The engine was still running. Other sounds emerged. Music blasted from the radio – an old favorite song of mine from the 80's, *The Killing Time*, which was ironic, but in that heart-stopping moment, I was not that reflective. All I could think of was getting out of there.

Panic hit me. Hard. I felt trapped, frantic to escape, and began to thrash about.

I groped for the red button on the seatbelt buckle, but my hands were shaking so badly, I couldn't push it.

My breaths came faster and faster.

I cried out, but no one heard.

Then suddenly, out of nowhere, a whip cracked. The vehicle shuddered.

I froze and tried to see past the smashed windshield in front of me. Everything outside the car was pure white, covered in snow.

If only I knew where I was. If only I could see something beyond the broken glass.

But it didn't matter what I could, or could not, see. I knew what was happening...

My car was sitting on its roof, resting on a frozen lake. The crack of the whip was the sound of the ice breaking.

Creak...Groan...

My SUV shifted and began to slowly tip sideways.

Large chunks of ice and bone-numbing swells of water poured in through the blown-out windows as I sank into the frigid February water. The shock of the cold took my breath away.

Frantically, I struggled with the belt buckle and managed, at last, to free myself, just as the last few pockets of air bubbled up to the surface.

I was completely submerged.

It was dark and murky down below. I couldn't tell which way was up, nor could I swim through the window, for a large shard of ice had become wedged there. I shoved at it with my shoulder, but to no avail. Then it occurred to me to open the door.

I groped for the handle and pushed it open against the weight of the water. Meanwhile, my body was going numb in the sub-zero temperature.

I swam toward the light, but collided with a thick ceiling of ice. No matter how hard I pounded against it, I couldn't break

through, so I swam, searching for the hole through which I
entered.

At last, I broke the surface and sucked in a great, gasping gulp
of air while I recklessly splashed about.

I struggled to clamber up onto the frozen surface, but my
body seemed made of lead. My teeth were clicking together. I
began to shiver violently, and then, by some miracle, I stopped
feeling the cold. My hands went numb as I made one last attempt
to claw my way up onto the ice.

Exhausted and disheartened, I had no more fight left in me.
My brain was shutting down. All I wanted to do was sleep.

I held on for as long as I could until my eyes fell closed. The
next thing I knew I was falling...

Down, down...

Slowly sinking toward my capsized car.

I settled lightly on the steel undercarriage, beside the muffler.

The rest of this makes no sense to me as I recall it, for my eyes
were closed – *I was not conscious* – yet I was able to see what was
happening from a location outside my body.

The convulsions and violent jerking of my legs were disturbing to watch. It was a seizure caused by the lack of oxygen to my
brain. I understood this with great clarity as I watched myself
twitch and finally go still.

Afterwards, I floated there for about twenty minutes, wondering if I should stay or go for help.

In the end, I decided to stay, because I just couldn't bring
myself to leave my body alone, in the cold, dark water.

A short while later, I squinted through the murky depths and
blinked a few times, for I thought I saw Megan swimming toward
me. How was this possible? As she drew closer, I realized that it

was not a hallucination. It really was my daughter, and I was no longer alone.

~⸜

A heavy splash startled me. I looked up and saw oodles of tiny, sparkly bubbles floating around a shifting black shape. It took me a few seconds to grasp that it was a scuba diver with flippers and a tank.

I darted quickly out of the way.

With quiet fascination, I watched as the diver scooped me up into his arms and carried me to the surface.

Megan was gone by then. She had said what she needed to say.

Twenty-one

The ambulance ride was strange. I looked quite dead on the stretcher – my skin was ashen and my lips were blue – but no one was trying to revive me with CPR or anything like that. They were only trying to keep me warm.

The female paramedic listened to my heart every minute or so with a stethoscope and kept shaking her head, but she told her partner that I wasn't really dead until I was *warm* and dead. She also mentioned that her own dog had been accidentally shot in the woods, trapped in snow for over an hour, but had made a full recovery.

I was surprised by that. I wanted to ask her more about it, but I knew she couldn't hear me.

The noise of the siren was startling. I wished the driver would shut it off.

At last, we arrived at the hospital. The ambulance doors flew open. The paramedics pulled my stretcher from the vehicle and the wheels extended to the pavement.

Suddenly there was a team of nurses and doctors all around me. With great efficiency, they rushed me inside.

According to Wikipedia, clinical death is "the medical term for cessation of blood circulation and breathing, the two necessary criteria to sustain life. It occurs when the heart stops beating in a regular rhythm, a condition called cardiac arrest."

That's what happened to me, almost a year after Megan passed from this world. I stopped breathing when I sank to the bottom of the lake, and I died there.

My circumstances, however, were outside the norm, for the reduced temperature of the water caused my blood pressure to drop, and all my systems slowed. Everything except for my heart and lungs continued to function, including my neurological activity – which didn't exactly explain why I was able to sit beside the paramedics in the ambulance and witness everything they said and did.

I wasn't questioning that, however. At least not while it was happening. It had all felt quite normal.

I was not in any pain, and the panic was gone. It had subsided completely after I left my body. I was no longer afraid of dying. All I felt was an intense yearning to go back to the lake and search for Megan. I wanted to see her again, desperately so, but I just couldn't seem to stray too far from my poor lifeless form on the gurney.

As soon as I was wheeled into the emergency department, the doctors and nurses set about bringing my body temperature back to normal, then they began aggressive cardiopulmonary resuscitation. I watched all of it from an elevated location in the corner of the room, just below the ceiling.

The head emergency doctor placed the defibrillator paddles on my chest and said, "*Clear!*"

Everyone paused and watched the monitor.

Perhaps that's when I re-entered my body. I can't be sure, but I do recall that I lost my breath for a moment. I zoomed through the air like a bullet.

Here, my memory fails me. All I can say is that I was no longer an out-of-body spectator, staring down at myself on the gurney. There was only darkness and silence, and I could think of nothing but what Megan had said to me at the bottom of the lake.

"*There are things you need to do, Mommy. Questions you need to ask. You can't be done yet. You need to forgive someone.*"

Who doesn't, I ask you?

Perhaps you should think about that, while you're healthy enough to do something about it.

Take my advice. Don't wait until you're dead.

Going Home

O n the day I left the hospital, the air was misty, the sky over-
cast. I passed through the hospital's sliding glass doors,
crossed to the parking lot, and looked up at the clouds,
which were hanging very low.

Surely this was some sort of miracle. How else could I explain
that I had died and seen Megan in the lake, and that she had
spoken to me?

Michael would never believe it. He'd probably call me insane,
which was why I had no intention of ever telling him. Besides, I
had business to attend to. Things I needed to sort out back home.

An ambulance siren wailed somewhere nearby. It rang in my
ears.

I wondered if I should have called my sister to drive me to
Camden. Surely I was in no condition to take care of myself.

Or maybe I should have called my father…

No. I wasn't ready to see him. At least not yet. There were
things I needed to do first. Questions I needed to ask. Megan had
been very clear on that point.

A blue sedan approached me, and only then did I realize I
was standing in the middle of the parking lot. I stepped gingerly
to the side, but the driver behind the wheel – an elderly man with
thick glasses and white hair – took no notice of me as he searched

for an empty parking space, spotted one, and carefully pulled into it.

I watched him get out of his car, shut the door behind him, and shuffle to the hospital entrance. He disappeared through the glass doors, and again, I was alone.

Panic came upon me suddenly. My heart jolted. I couldn't breathe.

Glancing back at the hospital entrance, I was half tempted to return and tell the nurses I wasn't ready to leave yet. I had been through a terrible ordeal and probably required some sort of anxiety medication, but I resisted the urge to go back inside. I may not have known what my future held, or how in the world I was going to navigate through it, but I did know one thing: I needed to return to the place where I had once been happy, where I had been a hopeful, optimistic person before the ground gave way under my feet.

I needed to return to my childhood home in Camden, where I would find the mother who had abandoned me twenty-three years ago. I needed to ask her the question I'd always wanted to ask, but had avoided all my life.

I clung to the hope that her answer would save me.

Megan told me it would.

CHAPTER

Twenty-three

❧

Camden, Maine

The morning broke in a menacing shade of grey, and the heavy scent of spring rain hung thickly in the air.

Eyes downcast, I walked through the downtown core of the small seaside village where I had spent the early years of my childhood. Camden had been my home until I was fourteen, but after my mother left town, Dad, Jen and I did the same. It's not surprising that Mom had now returned to our empty house. It was her birthright after all. She'd inherited it from her parents shortly after Jen was born.

As I watched the cracks in the uneven sidewalk pass by under my feet, it occurred to me that I was avoiding the sights and sounds around me. I suppose I didn't want to bump into anyone who might remember me. I was in no mood to explain what I had been up to over the past two decades, or why I had stayed away for so long, much less what I was doing back here now, ready to confront the woman who had broken my heart so long ago.

A motorcycle roared by, causing me to lift my gaze. Its engine sputtered foul-smelling black smoke. On the other side of the street, a chocolate Lab tied to a signpost barked at the obnoxious racket.

A man in a baseball cap hurried by. His hands were buried in his pockets. He looked tense and shivery.

Stopping in front of the soda shop, I moved a little closer to the window and cupped my hands to the glass. As I peered inside, I was suddenly affected by a wistful nostalgia, for almost nothing inside had changed.

How vividly I could recall climbing up onto those red vinyl stools as a girl. My father would always order my sister's favorite for both of us – root beer floats – though I preferred strawberry ice cream.

I recalled also, in spectacular detail, the man who owned the shop. His name was Max. He had a thick black mustache and always wore a blue striped apron.

At that moment, he emerged from the back room carrying a cardboard box. He, too, looked exactly the same. He bent to set the box on the floor, then reached for a cloth to wipe the countertop.

I could have lingered there for quite some time, simply reminiscing, but I had come home for a reason, so I continued on my way.

A short while later, I approached the house where I grew up – the white Victorian mansion that stood on a cliff overlooking the sea – and felt an uncomfortable stirring of emotion deep in my heart. I had been happy here once. When we were all together as a family, my world had been a place of joy and love.

Again, I felt the nostalgia I had experienced in front of the soda shop, and it surprised me, for I'd expected to feel only resentment upon my return. But somehow, the happy memories – and there were quite a few of them – eclipsed the more difficult events that had come later. I found myself wanting to dash up the stairs and burst through the door to my old room.

I worked hard to keep a clear head, however, and walked along-side the ivy-covered picket fence, pausing at the gate while I listened to the thunder of the waves crashing onto the cliff face below.

Much had changed since I'd last stood here. What had once been a wide green lawn with a stone walk to the front stairs was now an English garden. There was a trellis covered in vines, though the leaves had not yet sprouted. It was still too early in the spring, and everything appeared lifeless.

Such was the case with the large, rectangular flowerbeds, boxed in by rough-hewn logs with the bark scraped off. Nothing green flourished. There was only dark, wet soil everywhere, the occasional leafless shrub quivering in the fog.

I had never been one for gardens. They were too much main-tenance, and if you didn't do the work, the plants died or the garden grew to chaos. There would soon be too much chaos here, I thought.

At least the house looked well. Mom must have had it painted recently.

What was she doing now? I wondered.

My mother.

What was she going to say when I knocked on her door? What was *I* going to say?

Rubbing briskly at my arms to ward off the morning chill and prepare myself for what was about to transpire, I opened the gate. The hinges whined like an old cat as I entered the yard and started up the walk to the covered veranda.

When I reached the door, I knocked. It opened almost imme-diately, and there stood my mother, Cora, wearing that old famil-iar pink bathrobe with the little pompoms on the belt. I remem-bered it well. Her blonde hair had gone grey, but her eyes were still the same.

"Sophie." She hesitated briefly, and placed her hand over her heart.

Had she known I was coming? She didn't seem surprised.

"You're here." She paused again. "It's good to see you. I've been waiting a long time."

I found that hard to believe.

Anger rushed through me. Why did she leave us all those years ago? How could she have done that?

And why didn't Dad fight harder to make her stay?

For a brief moment, I was tempted to turn and leave before I started ranting. What was the point of this after all these years? Didn't I have enough turmoil in my life?

Something held me hostage, however. Perhaps it was Megan. She had told me to come here, and I couldn't let her down.

Also, I was curious. My five-year-old daughter had seemed to know a great deal about my life when she treaded water with me in the lake. She seemed exceedingly wise, more like a mother to me than a daughter.

I suppose she had experienced something very profound when she passed away – something beyond the scope of what I knew of this world, or the next. She had been gone a whole year, while I had been dead only briefly.

"*Why?*" I asked my mother, as I stood shivering on her front porch. I had come this far. I couldn't fail now to ask the question that had haunted me all my life. "Why did you leave us? Didn't you know how much damage you were doing?"

Her expression darkened with concern as she gaped at me. "*Why?* That's an awfully big question, Sophie. I think you better come inside so we can talk about it."

Taking a step back, she held the door open for me.

It was about time.

CHAPTER

Twenty-four

W hile my mother locked the door behind us, I glanced uneasily at the familiar floral wallpaper in the front hall, the mirrored bench with the tarnished coat hooks, and the ornately carved oak banister on the wide staircase to the left. It almost hurt to look at everything, for it took me back to the happy life I once knew, before it broke apart.

The house was quiet. There was no radio or TV blaring anywhere, only the sound of the sea, drifting in through an open window in the parlor.

I wondered how my mother could bear to live in this giant, old house all by herself, but remembered that she preferred to be alone, otherwise she never would have left us.

"Come into the kitchen," she said. "I was just about to make some tea. You look like you could use a cup."

Willing myself to behave in a civilized manner, I followed her.

The kitchen was painted a sunny shade of yellow with restored cherry cabinets and a new granite countertop. Green plaid valances framed the windows. Near the back door, there was a tall built-in bookcase for her cookbook collection that hadn't been there before. A few other things were different, too. Gone was the 1950s-era table with the sparkly white top and shiny chrome legs.

"When did you get this?" I asked, running my hand over the antique pine gem. "It's lovely."

"It is, isn't it?" she replied. "I always thought this old house needed some traditional pieces."

She was right. It was a Victorian. Aluminum furniture had no business here.

"Please sit down." Mom turned the knob on the back of the stove.

I rubbed my hands together and took a seat, wondering how long we would need to adhere to these polite rituals before she would answer my questions and talk to me openly about the past.

For a few minutes, I watched her putter about. She found the teabags and rinsed out the pot.

"It may surprise you to hear this," she said, "but I've always known what was going on in your life. Your father kept me informed, especially when Megan was ill."

My heart lurched with shock at this news, not to mention the sound of Megan's name upon my mother's lips. "He did? You and he kept in touch?"

He had never mentioned it.

"Yes," she replied. "I know how difficult it must have been. I'm sorry, Sophie. I'm also sorry that I never got to meet Megan when she was alive."

A painful lump lodged in my throat. I couldn't speak. It still hurt to talk about Megan, and the fact that my mother had been absent all these years and hadn't even sent a card after the funeral when she knew what was happening…That didn't help matters at all. I certainly didn't feel any responsibility to assuage her guilt.

She slanted a disapproving look my way. "I also know things have been awkward between you and your father. That you're not close, and you never visit him."

I shut my eyes and stroked my forehead. "You're a fine one to talk about not visiting someone, Mom. And please don't speak to me as if I am a child who is misbehaving. You gave up that right as a parent when you left us. So it's really none of your business how Dad and I feel about each other now."

Although that wasn't entirely true. I had come here to gain a better understanding about the relationships in my life. I wanted to know why she left. Why *everyone* left – Michael, and Megan, too. I needed to understand what happened between my mom and dad.

Why didn't he love me like he loved Jen?

I had an uneasy feeling that I already knew the answer to that. I'd *always* known it.

But did I really want to hear it now?

Mom set two mugs on the table and looked me straight in the eye. "I don't blame you for being angry, but you came here looking for answers, so if you want to hear the whole story, that makes it very much my business, because I'm the only one who knows the whole truth."

I leaned back in my chair and glanced toward the window. Outside, the ocean continued to hiss and roar as the waves crashed against the rocks.

"Did you know that he always disapproved of everything I did?" I asked. "He hated my friends. He told me I was too head-strong for my own good, and he never accepted the fact that I wanted to write. He wanted me to choose some other career. 'Something less creative.'" I shook my head. "He never treated me the way he treated Jen. She could get away with murder. He would have walked through fire for her, but he didn't feel that way about me." I met her gaze. "But *you*...You were the opposite, so I never understood why you left. I blamed Dad. It had to be his fault. It couldn't have been mine."

Mom sat down. "Your father is a good man, Sophie. I know you've had your differences, but he does love you."

I scoffed. "You really think so?"

Then I recalled our last telephone conversation when he had surprised me with his compassion. It was the first time he had ever spoken to me like that.

But then he didn't call again. Nor did I call him.

"If he's such a good man," I said, "why aren't you still married to him? Why did you leave us and never come back?"

Her blue eyes flashed with concern, and she hesitated before replying. "That couldn't be helped. Try to understand that. It's important that you do."

"Well, I'm sorry, but I don't."

The color drained from her face. "I should pour you that cup of tea now." She stood up and crossed to the stove. "Because we might be here a while."

I sat back in my chair and prepared myself, for it was long past time I knew where I came from. I needed to know the real story about my father.

And by that, I don't mean the man who raised me.

Cora's Story

"Sophie, I remember every precious moment your father and I spent together as if it happened only yesterday. I'm not sure where to begin. There's so much to say.

"I suppose I'll start with the summer of 1960, shortly after I turned twelve, because that's when things slowly began to change…"

It was the last day of summer vacation, and the first day I remember feeling differently about your father.

I finished my supper and rose from the table. "Thanks, Mom," I said. "I'm going next door."

Ignoring the sound of dishes clattering in the sink, I grabbed my sweater and dashed outside.

The sun was low in the sky, the air cool on my cheeks.

I hurried up Peter's steps and knocked on the door. His mother came to answer. "Oh, hello, Cora."

"Can Peter come out?"

She turned and shouted up the stairs. "Peter! Cora's here!"

He immediately came bounding down the stairs, grabbed his jacket from the coat tree and pushed open the screen door. It squeaked before snapping shut behind him.

"What'd you have for supper?" he asked, shrugging into his jacket.

"Pork roast. What'd you have?"

"Fried chicken."

"Lucky."

We both glanced down the street toward Matt's house. I wondered if he was still eating his dinner. His dad always made him do the dishes before he could play outside.

"Want to go out back?" Peter asked.

"Sure."

We ran around the side of the house, racing to the tire swing that hung from the big oak tree.

"You can swing first," Peter said. "I'll push you."

I climbed in and wrapped my arms around the tire. The old rope creaked along the tree bark on the overhead branch as he spun me in dizzying circles.

"*Stop! Stop!*" I cried, laughing and screeching, knowing I was going to be nauseous and dizzy as a goose the minute I hopped off.

Peter grabbed hold of my knees. "There. See? You're stopped." He grinned at me.

"It's about time."

I struggled to focus on his face. My head was spinning, but I could still see the yellow flecks in his brown eyes. His hands were warm on my knees.

I always felt so comfortable with Peter.

Just then, something caught my eye and my gaze darted to the side of the house.

"It's Matt," Peter said. There was a hint of disappointment in his voice.

My belly, however, was whirling with excitement – or maybe it was the after-effects of spinning in the tire swing. I wasn't sure. All I knew was that Matt had arrived and things were about to get exciting.

He sprinted toward us, flying like an airplane through the air, whistling like a torpedo.

Peter stepped out of the way.

"I'm hit! I'm going down!" Matt covered his heart with a hand and dove to the grass. He rolled a few times then came to a crashing halt, flat on his back, arms spread wide, directly under my feet. He lay very still, eyes closed.

Peter chuckled softly and shook his head, while I gazed down at Matt and laughed myself silly. "You're insane."

He opened his eyes and smiled up at me. His eyes were different from Peter's. They were a deep, cobalt blue – the color of an October sky.

"I will be by the end of tomorrow," he said, "because Mr. Hubert's gonna have it in for me, I know it."

Peter offered a hand and pulled Matt to his feet. "Well, don't do anything to get him riled. Just do what he tells you to do."

"You know I'm no good at that." Matt wiped the grass off the shoulders of his jean jacket.

Feeling energetic all of a sudden, I stretched my legs out and leaned back to start swinging again. Matt gave me a firm push, then another and another until I was swinging high and spiraling in great sweeping circles.

"Higher!" I shouted.

Matt pushed harder. The rope creaked along the thick branch. The leaves trembled and quivered. "I bet I can get you high enough to touch the top!"

Peter's gaze traveled up the length of the rope. "You better slow down," he said. "That branch is going to break."

"No, it won't," Matt replied.

"Yes, it will."

Matt grabbed hold of the tire and slowed me down.

"Let's go to the lake then," he said, then glanced down and noticed a grass stain on his knee. "Shit, my dad's gonna kill me."

"Want me to get a washcloth?" Peter offered.

"Nah. It doesn't matter. So what do you say? Want to go?"

Peter replied for both of us. "We're not supposed to go to the lake after supper."

It was a ten-minute walk through the woods, and our parents had a strict rule about that. Only in the afternoons.

"Ah, come on," Matt said. "Cora's parents and my dad know we're both here, and you can tell your mom we're all going to Cora's yard. They'll never know the difference."

It was true. They probably wouldn't, and I was tempted. There was no wind tonight. The water would be as shiny as a looking glass.

"It *is* the last day of vacation," I cautiously mentioned.

Peter spoke firmly. "No. It wouldn't be right. We'd get in trouble."

"Not if they never found out," Matt argued.

"But they might," Peter replied.

Matt shrugged, then swung his legs up over a branch to hang upside down by his knees. The ends of his wavy hair brushed over the grass. "My dad wouldn't care anyway."

I thought the opposite. Peter and I might get a scolding, but Matt would get a serious beating.

It was something no one talked about because Matt's father was a widower, raising his children alone. He'd been doing that since Matt was seven, after his mother fell down the stairs and broke her neck. The folks in town had whispered about it. They said her head turned around backwards.

My father was the town doctor, and he was the first to examine her when the ambulance brought her to the hospital, but he never spoke about it. For a long time afterward, I had nightmares because Matt's mother had been so beautiful, with long, black hair and red lipstick, and enormous, long-lashed blue eyes that always smiled. The thought of her dying like that had made me fear for the loss of my own mother at any given moment.

"Are we going or not?" Matt asked, his hair still sweeping the grass.

"No," Peter said. "We have school tomorrow."

Matt flipped forward and dropped to his feet. "That's a shame, because it sure is a nice night. I bet the lake is just like a mirror."

So that was how we were together, Sophie. Matt and Peter were my two best friends.

I realize now that I was the link that held our trio together. Without me, I doubt they would have been friends. They were two very different people.

About two years later, I was studying for a math test after supper, and after more than an hour of practice questions, I decided I was ready.

I closed my textbook and rubbed the sting from my eyes, then slid off the bed and crossed to the open window to inhale the fresh, salty scent of the sea air. Far in the distance, the sun dipped into the water and seemed to boil the waves on the horizon. I watched a sailboat cruise across the bay and wished I were out on my father's boat instead of indoors.

A familiar splash of red on the beach below caught my eye. It was Matt in his autumn jacket and denims, sitting alone. Writing a story, no doubt.

I let out a sigh. He, more than anyone, should have been studying for the math test. It was his worst subject, the one he disliked most of all.

Turning from the window, I reached for my blue cashmere sweater and pulled it on while I descended the stairs. A moment later, I was crossing the beach and climbing up onto the rocks.

"What are you doing out here?" I asked, taking note of the small coiled notepad on his lap and the pen in his hand. "You should be studying." I adjusted my skirt and sat down beside him.

"I did try," he explained, "but after about fifteen minutes I thought my head was going to explode."

"That bad?"

"Yeah."

We gazed out at the water. "So you came here instead. I can hardly blame you."

A soft breeze blew in off the bay. The waves were slow and lazy, foaming like soapsuds as they spread across the dark sand beach, then retreated.

I shut my eyes and inhaled deeply the familiar coastal smells that were such a part of my life – the salt and seaweed, the wet rocks and all the little washed up snails and jellyfish.

"You're lucky everything comes so easily to you," Matt said, draping a wrist across his knee. "You always do well in school, you get top marks. I wish I was smart like that. Maybe then my dad would be in a better mood."

"You *are* smart, Matt, in ways that I'm not."

"Like how?"

I glanced down at the notepad.

He stared at it, too, then flipped it closed.

"What's this one about?" I asked.

He leaned back on his elbows. "A kid who gets really bad grades."

I laughed. "I should have guessed. How does it end?"

"He drops out."

"Oh, no!"

Matt chuckled. "But then he meets a gorgeous older woman who hires him as a night watchman in an abandoned warehouse, and he writes about the things that go on there."

"Such as…?"

He grinned suggestively. "The woman drags a wooden crate into her office every night. She pulls it across the tiled floor from a room she keeps locked during the day."

"What's in the crate?" I asked, but he kept me in suspense for a few seconds.

"The bones of her dead husband."

I sat forward. "Did she murder him?"

"No, he died of natural causes, years before, but she couldn't accept it so she dug up his bones to keep them with her."

"That's gruesome, but I like it. Does she get caught?"

Matt squinted out at the water. "I haven't gotten that far yet, but I don't think so, and do you know why?"

I parted my lips, keen to hear the rest of the story.

"Because she's dead, too," he whispered.

"Dead?"

"Yes. Deceased, departed, gone to meet her maker – but she doesn't know it. She's been haunting the warehouse for years, looking for her husband who used to own the place."

I drew in a deep breath. "What about the boy who's the night watchman? Does he know his boss is a ghost? Is he scared? Does he tell anyone?"

Matt looked up at the darkening sky as he plotted the rest of the story in his head. By now, the sun had sunk below the horizon, though there was still a faint pink blush across the sky. It cast a dim glow upon Matt's face.

At last he looked at me. "No, he has no idea she's a ghost, but there's a reason for that."

I leaned forward again. "Tell me."

"Because he's a ghost, too."

My eyebrows lifted, and I smiled. "Promise me you'll let me read it when it's done."

"I always let you read what I write."

"But make sure you don't forget."

"I won't," he promised, flipping the notepad open again. He read over the last few lines he'd written.

The evening chill touched my skin, so I hugged my legs to my chest. A seagull soared freely over the water and cried to another. A rogue wave splashed onto the rocks.

Matt shrugged out of his red jacket. "Here." He slung it over my shoulders and put his arm around me.

I inched closer. "Thank you. It's getting cold."

We sat for a long time, looking out at the sea, watching the sailboat and marveling at the sunset. It was not the first time we sat together on the rocks, just the two of us, while Matt kept me warm. We had been doing it for years.

Peter knew nothing of it, of course, and it never occurred to either one of us to tell him. Maybe we knew that if he were with us, he would be bored unless we were up on our feet skipping stones. We would not be able to sit quietly, and to Matt and I it was pure bliss – to do nothing but stare out at the sea and listen to the waves, admire nature's artistry. It was the one place where we could forget all the noise and activity in the world, and all of life's hardships – which Matt knew so much more intimately than I did.

We had never questioned what our kinship meant. It simply existed. It never occurred to us that this closeness we felt – this inherent knowledge of each other – might lead to something more when we were older, because in those moments on the rocks, we lived only for the present.

CHAPTER

Twenty-seven

Spring 1964

"I'm worried about Matt," I said to Peter one day, as we stepped off the school bus and started walking up the hill.

"There's nothing we can do about it," he replied. "Matt knows what he has to do to get through this year. He just doesn't want to do it."

"But he might not grade, and if he doesn't...Well, I don't know what will happen. He'll never go to summer school. He might not ever graduate."

We walked slowly in silence, our shoes crunching over the gravel along the side of the road.

"I think he actually *likes* disappointing his father," Peter said. "It's his purpose in life."

I turned around to walk backwards, facing Peter and hugging my books to my chest. "Where was he after school? He wasn't even on the bus."

"He probably skipped class, like he's done every day this week. Doug Jones brought his dad's pickup truck today, and I heard they've been getting drunk in the woods down by the creek."

"That can't be true."

At that moment, the red pickup skidded around the corner at the bottom of the hill and sped toward us, leaving a cloud of dust in the air.

As they drove by, I saw Matt sitting in the middle between Doug and another boy I didn't recognize. Matt was drinking beer and smoking a cigarette.

"He didn't even wave," I said. "It's like he doesn't know us."

"He doesn't," Peter replied. "Not anymore. He has other friends and they're all up to no good."

I looked down at my brown leather shoes and hugged my books tighter. "But we used to be the three musketeers. Remember the time we took our bikes to the ridge? Or when we built the tree fort in the woods behind the old McKeown place?"

"Yeah."

"And the time you told his dad he was with us at the lake, when he'd been drinking down at the river? That wasn't all that long ago."

"I saved him a beating that day."

"He knew it, too. That was when he used to think we were his best friends."

All at once, I felt as if my heart was being ripped out of my chest.

Peter sighed. "People change I guess."

"How? I'm the same person I always was, and so are you."

"But *he's* not the same. He's gotten into some bad stuff."

I shook my head. "I don't believe that. He *is* still the same, and I feel like we should do something."

"You always wanted to save the world," Peter said. "But not everybody *wants* to be saved."

"It's not that." Why did Peter always have to be such a brick wall? Why wouldn't he listen? "If we could just let Matt know that we're here for him, and that we want to help. He's smart. He doesn't have to fail math and biology. Maybe we could have a study group or something."

Peter considered it, then shifted his leather book satchel from one hand to the other. "He doesn't want to try, and we can't force him. You know how headstrong he is. He doesn't care about school like we do. He doesn't care about anything. I reckon he'll drop out before graduation anyway."

Doug Jones dropped Matt off in front of his house, then skidded his tires as he backed up and drove back down the hill. Matt stood in his front yard, finishing his cigarette. He wore faded blue jeans and a black leather jacket, and he staggered sideways as he tipped his head back to blow a cloud of smoke into the air.

He didn't have any books with him. What was he going to do when he got to class tomorrow without his homework done? If he even made it to class.

Eventually he turned and climbed his rickety front steps. The screen door snapped shut behind him. A dog barked down the street.

I felt Peter's eyes closely scrutinizing my face.

"Feel like a swim?" I asked, struggling to sound more cheerful.

"Are you crazy? The water's freezing. There was ice on it barely a month ago."

I puckered my lips. "Yeah, well, it's hot enough to fry an egg on your porch today. Come on, why don't we? We'll be the first ones in after the spring thaw." I grabbed hold of his sleeve and dragged him the rest of the way up the street.

I knew I needed to forget about Matt.

"Why am I friends with you?" Peter asked with a chuckle.

"Because I'm your neighbor."

He was walking too slowly, so I turned around to walk backwards again. I let go of his sleeve and took hold of his hand instead. "Am I going to have to drag you the whole way?" I really wanted to go swimming. I wanted to feel the shock of the icy water on my skin.

"Probably."

I smiled at him. His hand was warm, and I remember thinking that this was no longer a boy's hand. He had grown tall over the past year.

There were rough calluses on his palm. I ran the pad of my thumb over one of them, then felt a strange fluttering in the pit of my belly.

Immediately, I dropped my gaze and let go of his hand, and he looked in the other direction toward his house. Feeling suddenly uncomfortable, I turned to walk beside him again.

Neither of us spoke for a moment or two, then Peter nudged me in the arm, knocking me sideways. "I'll race ya," he said, and the fluttering in my belly faded away.

"Not if I race you first." We ran up the hill.

I was breathing hard when we reached my gate. "See you in a few minutes?"

"Yeah, we'll meet back here."

I went inside to change into my swimsuit.

A short while later, we met out front and headed for the path at the top of the street, which would take us through the woods to the lake.

We rushed through the forest, running and laughing, leaping over exposed tree roots, ducking under low-hanging branches. It was a different world in the woods. The sea seemed a great distance away, almost non-existent. There was a quiet stillness in the air.

Soon we left the cool shade of the pines and emerged onto the sunny beach. I kicked off my sandals, while Peter hopped on one foot, tugging at a shoe.

"I can't believe I let you talk me into this," he said. He dropped his shoe onto the sand, pulled off the other one, then stripped off his shirt.

Suddenly aware of my heart beating faster as I stared at the muscles on his bare back and shoulders, I stopped unbuttoning my dress. Something had indeed happened to him over the winter. He'd not only grown taller, but thicker and stronger. He didn't look like the boy I always knew. He was different.

The next minute, he was sprinting into the water shouting, "Last one in is a rotten egg!"

But I hesitated. I couldn't seem to get past the third button of my dress…

"*Wooh!*" Peter broke the surface and flicked his hair back. Silvery beads of water exploded all around him. He laughed and wiped the wetness from his face, then stood up, shivering. He stared at me for a few seconds, then his smile faded.

"What's wrong?"

I cleared my throat and looked down. "One of my buttons is caught in a thread."

"Need some help?"

Suddenly I was shy. I couldn't even look at him. All I could do was keep my head down while I carefully unfastened one button at a time. "I got it. I'm fine now."

But I wasn't fine. I didn't feel like myself. Nothing seemed normal lately.

At last I unfastened the final button, shrugged out of the dress and dropped it onto the beach beside Peter's clothes. I picked my way barefoot to the water's edge and dipped my toe in.

"It's freezing!" I shouted with a smile. "Whose idea was this anyway?"

"Yours, and you're not getting out of it now." When I still didn't make a move, he frowned. "What's wrong with you? You've never been this slow before."

It was true. He knew me well. I was always the first one in – something I was rather proud of, considering I'd grown up with two boys for best friends.

But something was unusual that day, and I didn't really understand it. Was it because Matt wasn't with us, and I was worried about him? Or was it something else?

"Am I going to have to drag you in?" Peter asked.

"Hold your horses. I'm coming."

Clenching my fists and tensing my shoulders, I advanced forward, wading into the frigid water. When it reached the tops of my thighs, I sucked in a breath and dove under.

"It's like ice!" I shouted as I broke the surface.

Peter splashed me. "It was your idea, knucklehead!"

Then everything returned to normal, and I was relieved to feel like my old self again.

"Do you ever wonder if heaven really exists?" I asked Peter, as I lay on my towel next to him, watching the white cottony clouds drift slowly across the sky.

Peter rolled to his side. "No, I don't wonder that."

I shaded my eyes to look at him. "You don't wonder because you know it exists? Or you know it doesn't."

"I know it does."

I looked up at the sky again and laced my fingers together over my stomach. "How do you know? Have you ever been there?"

He chuckled. "No, but I go to church every Sunday, and I believe in God, so I have to believe in heaven."

"You *have* to?" I asked. "Someone is forcing you?"

"No. I just never question it, that's all. And I can't believe that *you* do. You sing in the church choir."

I watched a tiny cloud shift and roll toward the sun. "I suppose."

After a moment, Peter rolled onto his back again. "Why did you ask that question anyway? Are you worried about dying?"

"We're all going to die someday," I said.

"That's depressing."

"But it's true."

He turned his head to look at me. "Yeah, but it's a long way off, Cora. We've got our whole lives ahead of us, so there's no sense worrying about it now."

"Who says I'm worried?"

"You're the one who asked the question."

I leaned up on an elbow. "Would you feel better if I promised to worry about it later? When would be a good time? When I'm fifty? Or maybe sixty? How about seventy-five." I smiled.

He shook his head. "I don't really think you need to worry about it at all. What's the point? Because when you're dead, you're dead."

I slanted him a look. "But I thought you believed in heaven."

He stared at me, considering my point. "You think too much."

"And you don't think nearly enough. You're always so..."

"What?"

I paused, for I was having a difficult time trying to articulate what I felt. "You're always so at ease with things, just the way they are. Nothing ever makes you crazy or frustrated. You never seem to want to change anything."

"Why should I? Life is good."

"Is it?"

"Well...yeah." He pondered the notion for a few seconds, then sat up and twirled two fingers through a lock of my long blonde hair. "Especially now."

The strange fluttering in the pit of my belly returned, and my heart began to beat faster. We looked at each other in the warm sunshine, while I became more intensely aware of his bare chest and the way his damp hair fell forward around his face. I watched his lips as he wet them with the tip of his tongue, and realized that I was breathing hard, as if I'd just run a race.

He inched a little closer, then leaned forward.

My eyes fell closed as his lips touched mine. How soft and warm they were, not at all what I'd expected. His hot, moist breath beat against my cheek, and I could smell the outdoors on his skin.

The kiss lasted only a few seconds – seconds I knew I would never forget – then Peter drew back and gazed at me with a surprised look on his face.

"You just kissed me," I pointed out.

"Yeah. Are you mad?"

"No."

He was breathing hard, too. We continued to stare wide-eyed at each other until I had no idea what to say or do. I swallowed uncomfortably, and before I realized what was happening, he was leaning forward again and cupping my cheek in his hand.

Then he did it again – he kissed me – only this time he parted his lips and sucked a little on my mouth until my lips parted, too. Our tongues touched. The sensation made me sigh, and I was surprised at the sound, for it didn't feel like any noise I'd ever made before. It wasn't an unhappy sound. In fact, I quite liked the way his tongue tasted and the way it made me feel all weak and jelly-like inside.

Peter eased me down onto my back and leaned over me, kissing me more deeply, sliding his hand down the side of my bathing suit to rest on the top of my bare thigh.

I'd never felt anything like that before – such wild, heart pounding excitement. I reached out to wrap my arms around his neck and felt the smooth, contoured muscles at his shoulders.

He lowered his whole body onto mine. Then something pressed against my thigh. I drew in a breath of shock, and all at once felt pinned to the ground under the weight of him. Immediately, I slapped my palms to his chest and pushed. "Peter, stop."

He instantly rolled off me. "I'm sorry. I didn't mean to."

I sat up and hugged my knees to my chest. "It's okay."

We both stared straight ahead, across the lake. I listened to the ducks quacking, the fish splashing. I tried to slow my breathing and realized I was trembling.

"That was weird," Peter said at last.

"Yeah. I've never been kissed before."

"I know."

Of course he knew. He was my best friend. He knew everything about me.

But something felt very different now. It was awkward and uncomfortable, when it had never been before.

"Don't tell anyone, okay?" I said.

"You know I won't."

I believed him, because he was the most reliable person I knew. I would trust him with my life.

"We should probably go," he suggested.

He rose to his feet and offered his hand. I let him pull me up, then we dressed in silence. On the way home through the woods, we said very little. Only the sounds of twigs snapping under our feet and the occasional squirrel chattering from the treetops interrupted the dense quiet.

When we reached my driveway, Peter said, "See ya tomorrow," and kept walking.

"Yeah, see you at the bus."

And that was that.

For the rest of the school year and throughout the summer, neither Peter nor I ever mentioned what happened at the lake that
day. In July, we both turned sixteen, and Peter worked for his
father at the pulp and paper plant, while I scooped ice cream part-
time at the Lick-a-Split and put in volunteer hours at the hospital
and local animal shelter.

As for Matt, as soon as school let out, he left town without
saying goodbye. He went away to Chicago to live with his aunt,
but by then our trio had become a duo. Peter and I had grown
accustomed to it. We had given up on Matt.

And so, we carried on, swimming in the afternoons and riding our bikes to the same old places on our days off, going sailing
with my parents. Our friendship continued without awkwardness, as if the kiss at the lake had never occurred. Neither of us
ever mentioned it. It was completely forgotten.

The ice and snow was slow to melt that year, but in time, the sun bathed the earth in its warmth. The cold ground grew soft and warm, and the crocuses and daffodils appeared, smiling with pretty faces in the gardens. The natural world was growing and budding, coming alive with fragrance and color. Lilacs bloomed on tall, leafy hedges, the grass grew lush and green, and fresh spring rains pattered on the rooftops like a song.

Peter and I worked hard through the final days of school, turning in class projects, studying for exams and anxiously awaiting the first day of vacation.

"You're not going to believe what happened in fourth period," he said to me one day after school, as he joined me on the bench at the bus stop.

I was eating a chocolate chip cookie from my lunch box. Still chewing, I spoke through tightly closed lips. "What?"

"Susan Nichols asked me to the prom."

I had some difficulty swallowing. "You're joking."

"No. Can you believe that?"

"Does she *like* you?"

He chuckled in disbelief. "I don't know, I guess so. I didn't know what to say."

I dropped the half-eaten cookie back into my lunchbox.

I told myself I was not jealous. Peter and I were just friends. But still, I didn't like hearing that.

"You must have said *something*," I argued. "Did you say you'd go with her?"

"Of course not," he replied. "I don't want to go the dance with her." I exhaled sharply.

"I told her I was taking *you*," he continued. "Just as friends." He paused a moment and regarded me awkwardly. "I'm sorry! It just came out before I could stop it. I had to come up with something."

Our eyes met and I felt a surprising ripple of pleasure run through me. "So do you really want to go? For real?"

Neither of us had ever gone to a school dance before.

He shrugged. "I don't know. Do you?"

I shrugged, too. "People get dressed up."

"Yeah, and everyone gets talked about."

The bus pulled into the parking lot and spit out exhaust in a great hissing fit. We stood and moved slowly to the curb.

"Everyone knows we're just friends," he explained.

The folding bus door creaked open. We climbed aboard, said hello to the driver, and moved to the back. I sat down first. Peter swung in beside me.

"What would our parents say?" I asked.

"Your mom would probably like to buy you a new dress. She's always trying to talk you into going shopping."

"Yeah, maybe." The bus pulled away from the curb. "Matt would have a heart attack if he found out," I said.

"He won't. He's in Chicago, and who cares anyway?"

I gazed out the window. "Yeah. Who cares."

Our shoulders bumped occasionally as the bus rocked and swayed. For a long time we said nothing, then we talked of other things the rest of the way home.

Finally we reached the bus stop at the bottom of our street. "See you kids tomorrow," Mr. Hanover said, cranking the handle to open the door and let us off.

"Bye," I replied.

We hopped down and headed up the street.

"It wouldn't mean anything," Peter said, returning to the subject of the prom after the bus had driven away. "You'd just be saving me from going with Susan Nichols."

"How flattering. You sure know how to woo a girl." I smiled at him.

He grinned back at me with an appealing glimmer in his eye, and I wondered if he was thinking about that kiss at the lake. All at once, I became intensely aware of his masculinity – the way he carried himself and walked with an attractive swagger.

"All right, let's do it," I said. "We'll see what all the fuss is about, and we'll make fun of the decorations, and see who's going with who."

"With *whom*," Peter said, laughing. "It's a date then. Just friends, though."

"Of course," I replied, and punched him in the arm. "As if I'd say yes otherwise."

Over the next few weeks, I found myself completely swept up in the important task of searching for the perfect gown and shoes for the dance, and contemplating the all-important decision of how I was going to wear my hair.

My mother spared no expense. We went shopping together in the city, and flipped through dozens of fashion magazines, snipping out pictures and tacking them to the wall in my room. We talked about earrings and stockings and jeweled hair combs, stoles and pearls and different colors of lipstick. It was my first dance, after all. Everything had to be perfect.

But sometimes, when I was alone in my bed at night, looking out at the moon and listening to the stirring sound of the sea outside my window, I wondered what Matt would think of my prom date with Peter. If he had not left for Chicago, would he be going, too? Would we all still be friends?

⟶ᴄ

After a brief shopping excursion to Portland, I settled on a strapless, yellow chiffon number with a fitted boned bodice and rhinestones sewn into the skirt. On the night of the prom, my mother swept my hair into a stylish French twist. My long white gloves were silky upon my skin, and my mother's expensive perfume, which I had dabbed sparingly behind each ear, was the perfect finishing touch.

When the doorbell rang, I listened from the top of the stairs as Peter was invited in.

"Don't you look dapper," my father said.

"Thank you, sir," Peter replied. "It's a big night."

I descended the stairs, but stopped halfway with my gloved hand resting upon the rail. As soon as I saw Peter, my heart tripped over itself. How handsome he looked, dressed in a black-and-white tuxedo and bowtie. His hair was clean and tidily brushed. His black shoes were polished to a perfect sheen that reflected the light. I couldn't help but smile, and knew my cheeks were flushing red.

All eyes were upon me as I reached the bottom of the stairs. None of it seemed real. It was like a dream.

"You look beautiful," Peter said, and I was almost certain he was awestruck.

When at last I reached him, he handed me a corsage in a box. My mother helped me pin it on, then my father took our picture in front of the fireplace and drove us to the dance.

We gave our tickets at the door, and my heels clicked on the hardwood floor as we walked arm-in-arm down the wide hall to the gymnasium. The music from the orchestra grew louder as we approached.

"Are you ready?" Peter asked, pausing at the swinging doors.

Smiling at each other, we pushed through and stopped just inside, where we perused the gym in silence. Hundreds of tiny, white lights from a mirror ball swept over the walls like dancing starlight, and colorful paper streamers adorned the ceiling and concealed the basketball nets. The band on the stage played "Blue on Blue," and all the musicians wore black ties and clean white dinner jackets. There were only a few dancers on the floor, swinging each other around the room, but it was still early yet.

Peter and I took seats at one of the tables at the back and watched for a while. Other classmates soon arrived and joined us, and everything began to feel less formal once we were talking and laughing together.

Eventually we stood up to dance, and from that moment on, we never left the floor. When the last waltz began, I placed my hand on Peter's shoulder and felt the moist heat of his body through the thin fabric of his shirt, for he had removed his jacket earlier. His body was almost hot to my touch.

I, too, was perspiring. The balls of my feet stung inside my shoes. My cheeks were flushed and shiny.

When the dance ended, we stepped apart, but Peter did not let go of my hand.

"Thanks for bringing me," I said. "I had a good time."

"So did I."

Afterward, Peter's father waited for us in the parking lot, and we climbed into the back seat of his Ford. He dropped us off in front of my house, and Peter got out to walk me to the door.

I glanced at the front of my house and saw my mother in the parlor window, then turned my attention back to Peter. We stood for a moment outside my gate, cooling off in the evening breeze. We tipped our heads back to look up at the stars and listened to the crickets chirping nearby. Farther away, the mournful sound of the sea filled my head with desire. I felt a strange, unfamiliar longing.

"What a great night," Peter said.

"It was wonderful."

He gestured toward my front door. I flicked the gate latch and pushed it open, then started slowly up the walk. As my heels tapped over the flat stones, my toes throbbed inside my tight shoes. We climbed the steps to the veranda and stopped under the porch light.

"I guess I'll see you in church tomorrow," he said.

"That's where I'll be, just like always."

"And Wednesday's the last day of school."

I smiled. "Thank heavens."

We said nothing for a few seconds, while I looked down at my feet. My heart was beginning to pound. This was all very strange and not normal. I took a deep breath and swallowed, then Peter did what I knew he would do. He stepped forward, tilted his head to the side, and touched his lips to mine.

It wasn't like the last time. This kiss was more practiced. He seemed more certain of himself and what he was doing. I didn't think he'd kissed anyone since that day at the lake – if he had, he'd kept it secret – but I suppose he had time to think about it. This was no longer a first kiss. He knew exactly what he was doing. So did I – enough to relax a little and close my eyes.

Instinctively, I wrapped my arms around his neck. My breasts pressed tight against his chest as he slid his hands around my waist.

He held me close, then the kiss began to change. He parted his lips and met my tongue more aggressively. I let out a little sigh and the next thing I knew, he was backing me up against the front of the house and kissing the side of my neck.

Goosebumps erupted on my skin, and I could barely breathe from the thrill of it. But the kiss had to end. We both knew it. My parents were waiting inside...

Gracefully, Peter drew away. He was breathing hard, quite noticeably so, and gave me a sheepish look. "Wow."

I nodded in agreement.

"I guess I'll see you tomorrow," he said.

"Yes."

He started down the steps and passed through the gate, then turned around to walk backwards and wave goodnight, but stumbled a few steps. I laughed softly, and he laughed too, shrugging as if to say it couldn't be helped.

I can't deny that I was flattered. My insides were all aglow.

Turning away from him, I went into the house, closed the door behind me and leaned against it.

"Did you have a good time?" my mother asked.

"Yes."

I stood there for a long while, up against the door.

Then all at once, I felt as if I were being swept away on a fast ocean wave. I swallowed uneasily, and without another word to my parents, started up the stairs, reminding myself that there were no waves carrying me anywhere. This was simply my life.

The next day, while the minister spoke in church and I sat behind the pulpit with the choir, Peter and I continually locked gazes. Each time our eyes met, we shared a secret smile that caused my heart to flutter until I reined in my emotions and forced myself to behave. This was church!

The next time it happened, I sent him a stern and threatening glare because we both knew he shouldn't be looking at me that way – as if he wanted to kiss me again, and do a whole lot more.

That afternoon, we went swimming. There was a crowd at the lake, so any hopes for stolen kisses were quickly dashed, but on the way home, along the familiar path we had taken countless times before, Peter reached for my hand.

We said very little as we tramped through the forest. I was distracted by his touch and the pleasing heat generated by our hands clasped tightly together. When he stroked my knuckles with his thumb, I experienced a tingling sensation in the depths of my being and knew everything was about to change.

Sure enough, about half way home, he led me off the path to a private grove of junipers where we explored each other's untested desires.

The woods were quiet that day.

I couldn't hear the sea.

When summer vacation began, Peter and I returned to the jobs we had the previous summer. Peter worked for his father again while I scooped ice cream at the Lick-a-Split and volunteered at the animal shelter. I also became more heavily involved with the charity group at church, which collected for the poor.

Outside of those hours, however, Peter and I were inseparable, just as we'd always been as children, but everything was different now. The world seemed fresh and new to us, and we ended each night with a kiss on my porch swing – a kiss that lingered on my lips until bedtime.

Before long, we were kissing in other places, too – in Peter's living room when his parents weren't home, on the tire swing, at the movies, on my father's sailboat, and generally anywhere we could find a moment's privacy.

Though I was hesitant about certain, particular changes in our relationship, I did enjoy the kissing. I liked the sensation of his lips upon mine and the flavor of his tongue, and the way my body grew warm and aroused from his hands sliding up under my clothes. By summer's end, I felt less like a girl and more like a woman, and Peter seemed so much of a man.

We entered senior year as a couple, holding hands in the corridors between classes and attending all the dances, always together, never apart. Peter was now not only my best friend, but my lover as well – though not in every sense of the word, for I was determined to hold onto my virginity until I was married.

It was difficult, however, when Peter grew frustrated. I didn't like being a tease, but I couldn't resist his kisses either, and occasionally, in the back seat of his father's car or at the lake after dark, he wanted more. He would take things one step further than he had before, and often I would let him do it, but only to a point.

Thankfully, Peter was always a gentleman. He always stopped when I asked him to. He never pressured me, and I loved him for that. I would always love him. I knew that no matter what happened in the future or where destiny led us, he would never disappoint me.

He was decent and kind, unwavering in his integrity, which frightened me sometimes, because I wasn't always so sure I was as grounded as he. Peter was at ease with every aspect of his life and what lay ahead in his future. He knew exactly where he was going and what he wanted – to work in his father's pulp and paper plant and become a manager there someday. Eventually he would inherit the company. He would marry and have children. He would never leave Maine.

I, however, still had so many questions about the world. I often wondered if there might be something unexpected in my future. I imagined visiting different places, meeting new people. Sometimes, when I was alone in bed at night, I wished I could fly out over the moonlit sea and explore what was out of sight, just beyond the horizon.

Peter had no such desires, and I occasionally worried that one day, this difference in our natures might divide our path and lead us to very different destinies.

But that was the thing about the future. There was always plenty of time before it actually came upon you.

Flowers

CHAPTER

Thirty-one

❧

"I still don't understand any more than I did when I arrived," I said to my mother as I leaned back in my chair.

Mom had stopped talking and was staring out the window at the sea.

The fog had lifted. The sky was growing brighter now.

"You will." She slid her gaze back to mine. "When I'm finished telling you everything, you'll understand your father better. You might even be able to forgive him. But most importantly, Sophie, you'll see where you are at this important juncture of your life. You'll see what has been holding you back, and you might decide to do something about it."

I looked down at my empty teacup, wondering how this story could ever ease the impossible burden of my grief. It wouldn't bring Megan back. That much I knew. Nor would it change anything with Michael.

Not that I wanted it to. Our marriage was over, and I didn't want it back.

But could it change my relationship with my mother? Or would it help me understand why my father was always so distant and impatient? What Mom told me so far hadn't revealed any new insights. In fact, my dad was exactly the kind of boy I'd always imagined him to be.

"I need some fresh air," I said, sensing a sudden, somber dip in my mother's mood. "Can we take a break?"

"Sure." She picked up the teacups and carried them to the sink, then stood at the counter for a moment. "I should mention that I haven't told you what you really need to know yet, and it has nothing to do with your father. But I'm not sure you're ready to hear it."

I swallowed uneasily. "This is about *you*, isn't it? About why you left?"

All at once, I felt dizzy and nauseated. I experienced a flash memory of the day she walked out on us.

I was riding my bicycle through town, licking strawberry ice cream off my wrist. I could feel the grated metal pedals under the soles of my shoes. I could hear my squeaky wheels and the chain that needed grease. Quickly, I rounded the corner toward home, not knowing that my life would never be the same...

Mom touched my shoulder. "Why don't you go for a walk and get some fresh air? Besides, I need some time to get dressed."

I rose from the table. "Will you tell me more later?"

"Of course."

I turned from her and walked out the front door, where I paused on the covered veranda. I glanced briefly at the porch swing to my right, then breathed deeply the distinctive aromas of spring: the damp soil, recently thawed, and the mild, fresh air, wet and dewy after the rain.

It was still early in the day. The neighborhood was quiet. There was no one about, except for one woman across the street, a few doors down. She was outside in her yard, digging in the dirt with a small spade. She wore a wide-brimmed straw hat.

Gardening. When one had a garden, one had to weed it, and rake the dead leaves, and clean up all the fallen petals after the flowers bloomed and died. And what woman needed more work around the house? There was enough dirt to sweep and vacuum on the inside without getting into more of it on the outside.

Still, I couldn't deny an appreciation for a beautiful garden in full bloom, and I certainly adored the smell of roses and lilacs.

I watched the woman in the hat for a few minutes. There were no roses or lilacs in her garden. Everything just looked brown and wet.

The woman sat back on her heels and surveyed her work, then glanced up and saw me. She waved her arm through the air, as if she were trying hard to get my attention.

I glanced over my shoulder, wondering if she might be waving at someone else – we didn't know each other after all – but there was no one around, so I waved back.

She smiled brightly, and even from a distance, I felt a strange stirring of recognition. Perhaps I had met her before, many years ago. Perhaps I knew her from my childhood. Maybe we went to school together. She looked to be about my age.

Knowing Mom would need some time to dress and put on her makeup, I decided to go over and say hello. I started down the steps and crossed the street.

"Good morning!" the woman cheerfully said. Getting up off her knees, she placed a hand on top of her hat and smiled at me. She was strikingly beautiful with long black hair, a creamy complexion, full lips, and blue eyes.

I held out my hand "Hi. I'm Cora's daughter, Sophie. Have we met before?"

Still smiling, the woman removed her gardening gloves. She stepped forward to shake my hand, and I noticed two large mud stains on the knees of her jeans. "No, but Cora and I are very close."

I acknowledged the comment with a nod, and wondered what she must think of me. Surely she knew that I hadn't seen my mother in many, many years.

"I'm Catherine," she said, without the least sign of awkwardness. "It's wonderful to meet you at last."

"I just arrived this morning."

She chuckled. "I know. I was out here in my garden when you passed by earlier."

"Oh."

I hadn't even noticed her.

Too caught up in my own problems, I suppose.

"You have your mother's eyes," she mentioned, with a warmth of spirit that eased the tension in my neck and shoulders.

"I'll take that as a compliment." My mother had beautiful eyes.

I gestured to the garden bed at our feet. "I'm no expert, but aren't you starting a bit early?"

"Not at all," she replied. "The ground is soft, the sun is shining. The time is just right."

"I'm afraid I don't know much about gardening. I live in New York."

She linked her arm through mine. "That, my dear, is no excuse. Would you like a tour?"

"Um…" I glanced back at my mother's house. "I suppose I have time." I followed her to the flowerbed over by the fence.

"Right here, I'm going to have about fifty brown-eyed Susans," she explained. "They're my favorite flowers, but they won't come up until late summer, so I have some iris bulbs mixed in. Over here is my biggest hosta, which will be enormous by mid-summer."

We walked all the way around the house, and Catherine described every flowerbed in bright, colorful detail. It was a comprehensive garden tour – even though all I had seen so far was dirt.

We circled around to the front again, and I worked hard to summon my enthusiasm.

"It's going to be beautiful. I wish I could be here to see it in full bloom, but I'll probably be gone by then."

"Back home?"

I nodded, determined to hide the fact that whenever I thought of returning to my home in Washington Square, my insides churned with dread.

Life had been so painful there.

"Well…" Catherine paused. "When you have a life to get back to…"

"Me?" I chuckled bitterly. "I'm afraid I don't have much of a life, here or anywhere else."

Oh, God, did I really just say that? I sounded like such a whiner.

"Your daughter…" She nodded with compassion. "And your husband. I'm very sorry, Sophie."

So. She knew everything.

I inhaled deeply and let it out, and was at least thankful that I didn't have to explain why my life was such a train wreck.

And how nice to have someone speak the truth and not pretend that everything was okay, when it wasn't.

I looked down at the damp earth in the garden. "Obviously my mom told you about my recent setbacks."

"*Setbacks.* That's an awfully small word to describe what you've been through." She removed her hat. "And yes, mothers are always monitoring what's going on in their children's lives. Grandmothers, too."

I managed a melancholy smile. "I wouldn't know about that. I never knew either of my grandmothers. They both passed away before I was born."

"You have a sibling, don't you? A sister?"

"Yes."

"And you're close to her?"

"Yes."

"Well, that's a blessing."

I simply nodded.

We stood quietly for a moment, basking in the sunshine, then continued wandering about the yard. Catherine showed me where she intended to plant a rhubarb patch.

"Do you think you'll ever go back to work?" she asked. "I used to read your articles in the New Yorker. You're an excellent writer."

I was surprised to hear this. It had been years since anyone mentioned my work. "Thank you. It's very kind of you to say." I paused. "Funny…Sometimes it feels like it was all someone else's fairy tale." Because it was a different life, all gone now. "The truth is," I confessed, "I haven't felt ready to go back to work, or to do much of anything. Not since Megan…"

Catherine laid her hand on my arm. "It's completely understandable, Sophie."

"Is it?" I searched her eyes for answers. "Michael was ready to move on right away. He wanted to have another baby. He mentioned it just before Megan died. I remember wondering if he had a heart. I asked myself, 'Who is this man I married?' but now I wonder if I was the one who had no heart. Maybe it died with Megan, because I've been completely morose. I don't blame him for leaving."

The words spilled out of my mouth too quickly. They were like marbles, bouncing away in all directions. I wanted to chase after them.

Just then, my mother called to us from across the street. "Hello!"

"Good morning!" Catherine gave me a meaningful look that told me she heard everything I said, and that it was okay. Everything was going to be okay.

She waved at my mom. "I'm just showing Sophie my flowers!"

Struggling to collect myself, I glimpsed at the dirt. *Flowers indeed.*

"I don't think she's figured them out yet!" Catherine added with a grin.

"Figured them out?" I laughed. "Are they that difficult to understand?"

Catherine slid an arm around my waist and squeezed me affectionately. "Flowers can teach us many things, especially when they're out of sight, like these ones are, hiding in the ground."

She guided me out of the yard and back onto the street. "Now get back to your mother. She hasn't seen you in a while, and I know how much she's missed you. But please come back and see me again later. I would love to talk to you some more. Or if you want, I can just listen. I'm good at that. Actually, if you don't mind, I could use some help moving a shrub."

I laughed and nodded, then looked across at my mother standing on the veranda in a blue dress that I remembered from my childhood. It was long out of style now, but I appreciated her effort to take me back to the past with little details like the pink bathrobe with the pompoms, and now this.

I haven't told you what you really need to know yet, Sophie, and it has nothing to do with your father....

Suddenly I was impatient to hear the rest of her story and to discover this hidden truth she had promised me. Maybe it would help me find my way out of this dark cave I had retreated into, and back to a world where I was once happy and productive.

It was hard to imagine now, but there had once been a time when I rode the wheel of life as well as anyone. In fact, I rode it like a roller coaster at a theme park. It had *not* been a fairy tale.

On top of that, I had survived my worst nightmare. I was still here, wasn't I? Megan still believed in me. She knew I could fix this. She *wanted* me to.

So off I went, with a measure of hopeful determination I had not felt in a long time. I crossed the street and approached the gate, never taking my eyes off my mother's, while my heart began to pound in a curious, eager rhythm.

The Deep Blue Sea

Thirty-two

Cora

It was early October in 1968 when the monstrous wave crashed and exploded onto the coastline of my life, changing my future forever.

I had just turned twenty and was in my sophomore year at Wellesley College. Peter and I were still together. He was working full-time at his father's pulp and paper plant in Augusta and was being groomed to eventually take over the business when the time came.

In my senior year of high school, I had applied to a few colleges around the country, and as a result of my academic record and volunteer work, I was accepted into Wellesley with a full scholarship. I was so happy when I opened the letter from that illustrious school and read the news. I believed it would be my greatest achievement.

It wasn't, however. There was something else far more important in my future, but I knew nothing of that yet.

For two years, I studied cultures and humanity throughout the world, with a focus on Africa, Latin America and Asia. I completed courses in cross-cultural studies of family, gender, law, and economics, and in the fall of '68, I looked forward to graduating with a liberal arts degree in cultural anthropology.

Where life would take me after that, I had no idea. Most of the Wellesley women settled into married life not long after graduation. Some of them made quite spectacular marriages, in fact, for it was, at that time, the customary ambition for a woman of my age to become a wife and raise a family.

Perhaps that's why I was so distracted in my final year. I wasn't entirely certain I was ready to take that path.

On a very drizzly Tuesday afternoon, I remember sitting at my desk in my dorm room with a textbook open in front of me. I couldn't keep my mind on my studies, however. I kept glancing toward the window, where shiny raindrops pelted against the glass and streamed down in clear, quivering rivulets onto the stone sill. A wild wind outside was whipping the leaves off the trees and rattling the windowpanes.

Sitting there by the dim light of my flickering desk lamp and watching the violent weather outside put me in a pensive, reflective mood. I thought of Peter. I missed him, of course, but at the same time, all kinds of unsettling images of traditional domesticity began to flash in my mind like slide photographs on a screen.

A wedding dress. A three-tiered cake. Dinners, dusting, ironing, laundry soap, a burnt chicken in a roasting pan…

My heart began to pound as I sat there, trying so hard to study. I was aware of a growing sense of panic – a panic that quickly turned to desperation.

Frantic thoughts raced through my brain: *I was too young. I hadn't really lived. I wasn't ready to close all the doors in front of me and cross that matrimonial threshold.*

Peter, on the other hand, had no reservations about the future, not a single one. He doubted nothing, questioned nothing, and was simply counting the days until my graduation, when he assumed I would be ready at last to stroll down the aisle with a pretty bouquet of flowers in my hands.

He would have married me straight after high school if I hadn't had my heart set on college. He'd agreed to wait, only because he knew I needed to see and experience some of the world before I settled down. He knew it because he knew me better than anyone.

That didn't mean he understood it.

And so, I continued to sit there on that rainy afternoon, chewing on a thumbnail while I struggled with my anxiety.

It wasn't that I didn't love Peter. I did. I loved him very much. But for as long as I could remember, I'd felt a vague, mysterious longing deep inside me, which frustrated me, because even I didn't know how to satisfy it. For a while, I thought Wellesley would cure me of this mysterious yearning, but still, there it was, like the pull of a magnet around my heart.

Tapping the end of my pencil lightly against my lips, I looked down at the small print on the white pages of my textbook...

Then my telephone rang. It was the residence hall reception desk. "There's a gentleman here to see you."

A gentleman? I frowned with confusion. It couldn't be Peter. Unless he'd come to surprise me. But no, he would never do that. Was it my father? He hadn't mentioned he was coming by.

"I'll be right down." I stood up and checked the mirror quickly to make sure my hair was tidy and neat, then dabbed my nose with powder and smoothed out my skirt. I left my room and ventured downstairs.

—⟋‿⟍—

There, on the far side of the receiving room, a young man in jeans and a black leather jacket stood with his hands in his pockets, looking out the window. I didn't recognize him, not at first, until he turned around and a quiver of excitement surged through my veins.

Matt.

I sucked in a breath and laid a hand over my heart. It had been almost six years. There had been no word from him, and I had accepted quite some time ago that I would probably never see him again. I'd even made a sincere effort to push every memory of him from my mind, for it was painful sometimes to think about our close friendship.

But there he was, in the flesh, standing in my dormitory at Wellesley College, his thick, black hair wild, unruly and wet, his eyes just as deep and blue as I remembered. There would be no pushing this image away. Not ever.

"Hey," was all he said.

His gaze traveled slowly down the length of my body. He looked down at my black leather shoes for a long moment before he finally lifted his gaze.

Managing a few shaky breaths, I walked toward him. "My goodness," I said. "I wasn't expecting it to be *you*. What are you doing here?"

Then suddenly I was *ecstatic* to see him. He looked so different. He seemed to have aged a lifetime. He wasn't sixteen anymore. He was a man.

He shrugged, then smiled that mischievous, crooked smile, his eyes gleaming, and I knew he was ecstatic to see me, too, even though his posture was relaxed. I could feel it somewhere in the mix of my out-of-control emotions and the clear, vivid memories of our childhood together.

My cheeks flushed with heat. I crossed the remaining distance in three long strides and finally stood before him. "Matt... The last I heard, you were in Chicago."

He studied all the details of my face. "That's right, and I'm still there. I'm just visiting right now, staying with my brother in Boston."

"Well, that's wonderful." I wasn't quite sure what else to say. My brain was turning to mush.

We stared at each other for a few seconds more, and despite feeling completely incoherent, I couldn't believe how happy I was just to see him.

"You look great," he said in a soft voice.

I couldn't help myself. I stepped forward, wrapped my arms around his shoulders, and pulled him into my arms. He immediately buried his face in my neck. The leather of his jacket creaked like an old ship under my hands. He smelled of musk and rain.

"It's so good to see you," I whispered in his ear. "We've missed you."

And there it was. The *we*. I wasn't sure why I had said it. I hadn't meant to inform him of anything. It just came out.

Slowly, he released his grip on my waist and looked me in the eye as he stepped back, nodding as if to say he understood, when I hadn't meant for him to understand anything.

"So you and Peter are still close?"

"Yes." I felt awkward all of a sudden. I wished I hadn't said *we*, but it was such a habit. "I wasn't sure if you even knew about us, that we'd been..." I paused. "We've been together for a while. You've been gone so long."

Matt casually slid his hands back into his pockets. "I know. I talk to my father every once in a while. He always tells me what's going on back home."

I moved to the sofa and sat down. Matt took the chair across from me. He sat forward and rested his elbows on his knees.

"How are things with your father?" I asked, because I remembered it was why he'd left Camden in the first place, even before finishing high school.

"Better now that we're not living in the same house. Or the same town, for that matter."

I nodded. "I'm glad to hear it."

Matt leaned back in the chair and stretched out in a lazy sprawl. "I know I used to say I hated him, but..." He glanced around the room. "He just had it rough, that's all, trying to raise all of us on his own. I can see that now. Though I don't know if he's any different than he used to be. He's probably the same."

"It couldn't have been easy for him after your mother died," I replied. "It couldn't have been easy for any of you."

I'd never said anything like that to Matt before. It wasn't something children said to each other.

"Do you have a job in Chicago?" I asked, sitting forward and resting my chin on a fist.

"Yeah, I'm working for a construction company right now."

"Doing what?"

"Construction." He grinned.

I smiled in return. "I see *you* haven't changed."

"Oh, I think I probably have."

I was tempted to ask why, or in what way, but refrained because it seemed too personal a question after so many years apart.

"Tell me more about your job," I enquired. "Do you drive a forklift? Fill out invoices? Pour cement?"

"I do a bit of everything, except the invoices. Most of the time, I'm swinging a hammer, or raising a wall."

That, I could see.

"Do you enjoy it?" I asked.

"It's a living."

I sat back and said nothing for moment or two. "I always wondered what became of you after you left."

He looked down at his index finger, which he was tapping on his knee. "Not much of anything, I suppose. Except that I did finish high school. That was the deal with my aunt. She told me I had to finish, and if I failed just one test, she'd send me back home to Dad."

I nodded. "So you passed everything, I presume."

"With honors."

"Really." I was so pleased to hear it.

The front door of the residence hall opened, and a group of five freshman girls came dashing inside to escape the wind and rain. Squealing and laughing, they brushed the water from their coats.

"Hi, Cora," one of them said, sneaking a curious glance at Matt.

They were wondering where he'd come from no doubt, for he was impossibly handsome in a James Dean sort of way. He looked nothing like the young men who came around Wellesley with their short haircuts, crested blazers and neckties.

Yes, there was something dangerous about Matt. There always had been. He wasn't the kind of boy a young girl's mother would be pleased to meet.

The freshmen girls climbed the stairs and entered a room upstairs. I wasn't sorry to hear their squeals die away with the click of a door.

I met Matt's deep blue eyes again.

"Have you made a lot of friends here?" he asked, looking around at the traditional decor – the Victorian furniture, the chintz curtains, the gilt-framed portraits on the papered walls.

"A few, but I'm older than most of them in this dorm, so we don't have much in common. I stay in a lot."

"Because you have a boyfriend back home," he added, but it seemed more of a question than a statement.

I sat back. "It's not just that. I spend a lot of time studying. I might want to travel next year, to some of the countries I've been learning about."

I didn't know where that had come from. I had never before committed to any future plans beyond graduation, nor even hinted at such a thing. I couldn't imagine what Peter would say.

Matt sat forward slightly. "Yeah? What countries?"

I answered the question as if I'd already given it a great deal of thought. "I'd like to see Africa."

"Africa." He leaned back again and tapped that finger on his knee. "That would be great." He paused. "So how is Peter? He must still be working with his father?"

"That's right."

"We always said that's where he'd end up. Remember?"

I smiled, pleased by this acknowledgement – however small it was – that we had been close at one time and understood each other's minds.

Another group of girls pushed through the door and giggled into the reception room. When they noticed Matt, they went silent.

Unlike the others, they quickly disappeared up the stairs without a word.

"Busy spot," he said.

"Want to go somewhere?" I immediately suggested. "We could get a drink or something. I just haven't seen you in so long...I'd love to hear more about Chicago."

"Yeah, sure," he replied. "Where do you want to go?"

"There are a few places in the village. Just let me get my coat. I'll be right back."

I hurried up the stairs to my room, threw on some lipstick and brushed my hair, and realized with quite a bit of uneasiness that I couldn't remember the last time I'd felt so wound up.

I grabbed my handbag and coat, and trotted back down the stairs.

Matt was waiting by the front door, flipping his keys around his finger. "Ready?"

"Yeah."

He held the door open for me. Outside, the wind was gusting through the trees and the rain was coming down sideways.

I pulled my coat over my head. "I'm glad you have a car."

"Though we might need a rowboat if this keeps up." He pointed toward a silver and black hardtop with shiny metal trim. "That's my brother's Buick over there. Come on."

He took me by the hand and we dashed across the courtyard, splashing through puddles. He unlocked my door and held it open while I climbed in, then slammed it shut, ran around the front of the car and slid into the driver's seat.

"Now *that's* what I call a downpour." He flicked the water out of his hair.

I laughed and tried to wipe the wetness from my cheeks, but my fingers were wet, too, so I rubbed them on my knees.

"It is an absolutely *perfect* day," I said, smiling. "I wouldn't change a thing."

I reached into my handbag for my compact, and while I checked my makeup in the little round mirror, I was intensely aware of Matt's eyes on me.

"You're staring at me," I said at last, as I snapped the compact shut.

"Yeah, I am."

I met his gaze, but he didn't look away. He continued to stare, and for a few brief, electrically-charged seconds, I gave into that old familiar connection that existed between us when we were children – when we would smile at each other as if we could read each other's minds.

So much about him was the same: the expression in his eyes, the quiet intensity, the way he made me feel as if he were holding me in his arms, though we weren't touching.

But there had always been an inexplicable understanding between us, as if we were swimming together in the same pool of thoughts and desires and ideas, just the two of us. Sometimes, as a child, I felt that he was my other half, even though we were two very different people. When I dreamed at night, he was always a part of those dreams.

He looked away and slipped the key into the ignition, and the connection between us snapped like a taut cord. In that moment I realized, with more than a little regret, that while he was the same in many ways, there were changes in him as well.

Where he had once been angry and wild as a youth, he seemed calmer now. There was something different in his eyes. A look of defeat, I wondered?

Or was it peace? A sense of easiness with the world and his place in it?

I faced forward, contemplating the strange aching sensation in my chest.

I suppose we had lived apart for too long. There were things I didn't know about him, when at one time I knew everything. The years felt like a deep chasm between us.

He turned the key and started the car. The engine roared. The wipers batted noisily back and forth across the windshield as the rain rapped upon it.

"Where to?" he asked.

I pointed. "Just take us in that direction, then you can turn right onto Central Street."

We drove across the campus, saying nothing while I looked out at the blustery weather outside. We drove past rolling green hills strewn with the first fallen leaves of the season, and past wooded groves of conifers and ancient oaks. The brick-and-stone university buildings – cloaked in green ivy with leaves quivering in the storm – always reminded me of old English manor houses, straight from a fairy tale.

That moment felt like a fairy tale, I thought soberly. A stormy, tempestuous tale, full of uncertainty and regret.

Or maybe it was more like a hallucination, and in the morning I would wake and discover it was all nothing more than a dream.

❝I t's a nice campus," Matt said.

We stopped at an intersection. The rain pounded on the roof of the car, while the wipers squeaked intermittently across the glass.

"How long will you be visiting your brother?" I asked.

My gaze was transfixed by Matt's hands on the wheel. They were thick, strong, callused hands – the hands of a builder – and yet I remembered so clearly how they had once held a pen...

"Not very long," he replied.

I turned toward him. "*How* long?"

"A week or so. Gordon bought a boat a couple of years ago, and he's letting me take it out before he brings it in for the winter."

"He has a boat? What kind?"

"A sloop. Thirty-six feet. It's at Marblehead."

I tipped my head back on the seat. "That sounds great. I haven't been sailing since high school. Can you believe that?"

He looked at me with surprise. "Why not?"

"Dad got rid of the boat last year. He wants a new one. So you're on vacation just for this week?" I asked.

"Yeah. My boss is really good. He gives me time off whenever I need it. I don't get paid for it though."

"You can pull over right here." I pointed toward an empty parking spot on the main street.

Soon we were out of the car and splashing through puddles again, ducking through the rain, hurrying into the pub.

The door swung shut behind us. Inside, it was warm and dry and smelled like stale beer.

It was quiet for a Saturday. There were only a few people in the circular booths along the side wall. One older man sat alone at the bar hugging a tumbler of whisky in both hands. The bartender was filling two glasses of beer at the taps.

I removed my coat and followed Matt to the back, where we slid into a booth. The waitress came by and took our orders. As soon as she was gone, we sat forward and folded our arms on the table.

"It's so good to see you," I said.

"You, too."

"Are you still writing?" I had been waiting until now to ask.

He casually shrugged. "Here and there. I sold a short story to a magazine a couple of years ago."

"No kidding. That's great. Was it a story I would know?"

A stupid question. I hadn't read anything of his in years. It was probably something he'd written after he'd left home.

"No," he replied. "I don't know where all those old stories are. In a box somewhere I suppose, unless my dad burned them. Anyway, I was just a kid then. I can't imagine they were any good."

"I thought they were. So you wrote this story in Chicago?"

He nodded.

"I'd love to read it sometime. Do you have any copies of the magazine?"

"A couple."

"Will you send one to me?"

"Sure."

"Promise me," I firmly said.

"I promise."

Our beers arrived, and we clinked glasses.

"To old friends," I said.

"Old friends."

We both took generous sips, and I discreetly wiped the foam from my upper lip.

"Have you written anything else lately?" I asked.

He set down his glass. "I started a novel a couple of years ago, but I haven't finished it."

"Why not? You should."

"We'll see." He leaned back and stretched his arms over his head, staring at me mischievously. I felt that old spark of excitement that came from not knowing what he was going to say or do next.

"So you and Peter…" he teasingly said, as if they were twelve years old again. "He always did have a thing for you, even when we were kids. He used to watch you from his bedroom window, you know."

"He most certainly did not!" I made sure to convey the proper degree of shock, even though I was fighting not to laugh.

"I caught him at it once." Matt picked up his beer and toasted me, as if to say "no joke."

I was still smiling. "Well, nothing happened between us until after you were gone."

He swallowed a big gulp. "Either way, I always knew you'd end up together. It was inevitable."

"Why do you say that?"

"You couldn't have ended up with *me*. God help you if you had."

I leaned closer and found myself staring at his lips. "That's poppycock."

He looked at my lips, too, then spoke earnestly. "It's the truth and you know it. You were lucky Peter was always around to keep you out of trouble. Without him, you and I might have gotten into a few scrapes, because we both know I was a bad influence." He squinted at her. "And you were always teetering right on the edge."

The waitress came by. "How is everything?"

"It's fine, thank you," Matt answered, while I remembered those long ago days.

I lifted an eyebrow and spoke in quiet, husky voice. "So are you *still* a bad influence?"

The small crowd at the booth behind us exploded with laughter, but Matt and I never took our eyes off each other.

"In some ways, maybe," he replied. "In other ways, no. I had to grow up eventually."

As did I, because we couldn't ride our bikes around town and spin on tire swings forever.

I took another sip of beer.

"You've done well, Cora," he said. "You should be proud."

"I guess."

"You *guess*? What's there to guess at? You earned a scholarship to one of the best schools in the country."

The jukebox flipped a record and began to play.

When I didn't answer, Matt leaned forward. "*Talk.*"

"It's complicated," I tried to explain.

"How?"

I realized I was looking at his lips again, studying all the moist creases. "Everything seems perfect on the surface," I told him, "but sometimes I feel like I don't know what I'm doing, or where

I really want to be, and I've always had this strange unexplainable urge to escape from wherever I am, because nothing seems quite enough, and I feel incredibly frustrated sometimes, like there's more to life out there somewhere, but I don't know what it is, or where it is. Do you ever feel that way?"

I had never said any of that to Peter. I couldn't imagine it. He would never understand.

"You have no idea." Matt spread his arms wide. "Look at me. I've screwed up plenty in my life so far, and I know what everyone thinks – including you. That I didn't live up to my potential, that I could have been so much more if I'd only applied myself. You don't know how many times I've heard that, and now, sitting here at the ripe old age of twenty-two, I know that everyone was probably right. I could've done more, been more, but I didn't, and I'm not. Now I have to accept that I never really accomplished anything. So yes, I feel frustrated, more than you know."

The people at the table nearest to them rose from their chairs, pulled on their coats, and chatted while they walked out of the pub.

"You sold a story to a magazine," I said. "That's something to be proud of. And you enjoy your work, don't you? Building houses?"

"I like it enough. But there are other things I wish I had done differently. Maybe I should've…" He stopped and shook his head. "I don't know. There's no point in having regrets, is there? All they do is eat away at you."

I was surprised we were saying all this to each other before the food had even arrived, when we hadn't spoken in almost six years. Anyone who knew our history would call us strangers now, but at the same time, no one – not one single person in the world – could ever *really* know our history.

A memory flashed in my mind, of how it felt to sit with him on the beach with my head on his shoulder and his arm wrapped around me while we listened to the surf. I remembered it as if we had done it only yesterday, and could almost feel his arms around me – all the same emotions, the easiness and contentment. I was tempted to slide along the half-moon seat and link my arm through his.

"It's never too late," I said, struggling to remember my situation, "to turn your life around, Matt. You're only twenty-two. You can still do something more, once you figure out what it is you want to do, whether it's to write novels or something else. That's the hardest part, I think. Figuring it out. I'm not sure I have yet."

He stretched his arm across the back of the seat. "You said you want to travel."

"Yes." I lifted me eyes. "And maybe I will."

"Don't say maybe. Just do it. Life's too short. You don't want to look back on everything someday and regret all the things you didn't do. You said yourself that you were frustrated. Go find out how to fix that."

There was a clatter of cutlery and plates as the waitress cleared a table on the other side of the pub.

"Maybe *you* need to do that, too," I told him.

"Maybe I'm doing it right now," he replied.

My heart began to beat erratically. "How so?"

"By coming back here. Seeing you."

I sat motionless, staring into his clear blue eyes. All I wanted to do was reach out and touch his hand, but instead I wrapped my hand around my beer glass and took a long, slow sip.

The waitress arrived with our meals and set them down on the table. As soon as she was gone, Matt reached for the ketchup bottle.

"You look pale," he said.

"Well this is strange, being here with you."

"Why is it strange? We're old friends."

I picked up my fork and poked at my French fries.

We were quiet for a long time, and I swallowed thickly over a lump that had lodged in my throat.

"Maybe I shouldn't have come," Matt said, sitting back.

Terrified suddenly that he was going to suggest he drive me back to the dorm right now and be on his way, I jostled for the courage to say what was really on my mind.

"No. I'm glad you came. I've thought about you so many times over the years, even though I tried hard not to. I've wondered about you and hoped you were happy. Have you been? Apart from being frustrated, I mean."

He gazed at me intently. "You want the truth?"

I nodded.

"Then the truth is no. I've never really been happy."

His answer cut me to the quick. "Why not?"

"Too many regrets."

I swallowed uneasily. "I have some of those, too."

He looked at me for a long time as if he understood, but it was pointless because there was nothing to be done about it.

Was it true? Was there really nothing to be done about regrets?

We sat together in silence after that, eating our dinners without talking, while the rain outside continued to fall.

"Do you have a girlfriend?" I asked after a while when the jukebox stopped playing. It was a bold question, but I wanted to know.

"I've had a few over the years," he said. "Nothing to write home about, though. But you and Peter, you've been together for a while."

"Yes." I paused. "He's waiting for me to finish school so I can come home and we can get married."

Matt tilted his head to the side. "You're engaged. Officially?"

Another bold question.

"No, not officially. I don't have a ring on my finger or any-thing – at least not yet – and I'm still not completely sure it's the right thing."

"Do you love him?"

I had a hard time swallowing. "Of course I do. It's Peter we're talking about."

Matt nodded, then dug into his pocket for some change, slid out of the booth to go to the jukebox.

I watched him walk across the bar and stand before the list of songs, then let my eyes wander down the length of his body, from his broad shoulders beneath the black leather jacket to his narrow hips in those loose, faded blue jeans. He was as handsome as ever. I couldn't take my eyes off him.

He dropped a few coins into the slot, and they clicked down through the metal machinery. I closed my eyes and listened to the sound of the record flipping over and the needle touching the shiny black vinyl. "Smoke Gets in Your Eyes" began to play.

When I opened my eyes again, Matt was in front of me with his hand out. "Dance with me."

Compelled to rise to my feet, I followed him onto the small dance floor. There was no one else in the bar now except for that old man hugging his whiskey.

My heart began to pound as Matt slid his arm around my waist and took hold of my hand, pulling it close to his chest. Gently, he stepped nearer, and I became aware of the heated rush of blood through my veins. I made every effort to commit to memory each sensation – the texture of his soft leather jacket where my hand rested on his shoulder, the feel of my lips close to his hair.

We moved slowly in rhythm to the music. Neither of us exchanged a word until it was over, and the jukebox clicked and flipped another record onto the turntable.

We stepped apart.

"The truth is," I said, "I'm not even sure I want to get married. At least, not yet. There are so many things I want to do and experience. I don't think I'm ready to just be a wife."

"Cora." He eyed me intently. "Whether you get married tomorrow or ten years from now, you will never be *just* a wife. You'll always be you."

I smiled at him. "Thank you."

After we returned to the table, we began to talk of other things – my college classes, Matt's job, our families. We split a piece of apple pie and lingered over coffee, talking and catching up on everything until the waitress approached with the bill.

We checked our watches and realized we'd been sitting at the table for four hours.

"Oh, God!" I exclaimed. "I have to get back before they lock the doors."

"What if you don't?" He grinned suggestively.

"Let's not even think about it."

As I gathered up my coat and handbag, I tried to remember a time in my life when the minutes and hours had passed so quickly. I thought of all the times I had gone for dinner with Peter. Very often we would sit in silence, watching other people eat, talking about the food but not much else. We had never spent four hours over a meal, not even when we'd first become a couple. We would spend time together walking or going places, but there was always so much silence.

Matt paid the bill and we left the pub. Outside, the rain had stopped. The air was fresh and mild. Streetlamps cast white reflections in the shiny dark puddles.

"Will you go back to your brother's place now?" I asked as we walked to the car.

"Yeah." Matt helped me into my seat, then circled around to his side. He got in and started the engine. A few seconds later, we were heading back to campus.

As we drove through the dark, quiet town, dread settled heavily in the pit of my stomach. He was going to drop me off, say goodnight, then I might not see him again for another six years. Or maybe never.

He flicked the blinker to turn onto the campus, and my heart began to race with panic. I felt almost sick to my stomach.

I laid a hand on his arm. "Don't turn yet. Why don't we keep driving for a bit?"

His gaze shot to my face. "What about your curfew?"

There was tension in his brow, as if he were experiencing the same horrible, gut-wrenching dread.

I held my wristwatch up to a streetlamp as we passed under it. "We still have some time. Not much, but a little."

Matt took his foot off the brake and pressed on the gas. "Where do you want to go?" His voice was low and serious. "Just tell me which way."

"It doesn't matter," I said. "Just drive."

Without a word, we continued west along Central Street. Every so often, Matt angled a glance at me. I met his eyes in the dark car and felt as if we were fugitives fleeing a crime, with no clue where we were going.

I tapped my heel repeatedly on the floor of the car – *tap, tap, tap* – and clutched my handbag on my lap. I twisted it, wrung it, squeezed it.

"What are we doing, Cora?" he demanded at last, when we seemed only to be following the white headlight beams into the darkness.

"I don't know." We had no particular destination, and it felt wrong. "Maybe you should just pull over."

He turned onto the shoulder of the road, where the tires crunched over the gravel, then he switched off the engine and lights.

The world – and all the raging thoughts crashing around inside my brain – suddenly grew quiet. Matt rolled down his window and rested his arm on the door. The cool night air drifted in, and I took a deep, cleansing breath. Crickets and frogs chirped in the wet ditch. Moonlight streamed in through the front window. We were surrounded by trees.

"Why did you stop talking to Peter and me back in high school?" I asked, feeling angry as I pushed my hair away from my face. "What was so special about Doug Jones and his old pickup truck? Was he more interesting than we were? Were you bored with us?"

The question had nagged at me for too long. I had bottled up that rejection years ago and stuck a cork in it, hidden it away. Now it was bubbling over.

He took his hand off the wheel and turned toward me. "I wasn't bored. I just knew I was different from the two of you. I was fed up and headed for trouble. You were better off without me."

"We didn't believe that. At least I never did," I insisted. "We were friends, no matter what, and maybe if you had stayed with us, you wouldn't have gotten into trouble in the first place, and you wouldn't have..." I stopped.

"Wouldn't have what? Left town?" He gazed out at the night. "I needed to be on my own," he explained. "That's all it was. I had to get away from my father, who took some kind of perverse pleasure in beating the crap out of me." He paused. "I just couldn't be part of that group we'd become."

"But you joined another group – Doug and his idiotic friend. I don't even remember his name."

Matt shook his head. His eyes held no expression. "They were both assholes. I never thought otherwise."

"Then why were you friends with them? Why not us?"

God, I sounded like a pathetic, spurned lover, as if he had cheated on me and abandoned me. But I was not his lover. It had never been that way between us.

But what was it, exactly? There had never been a word for it. There still wasn't.

I covered my forehead with a hand and shut my eyes. "I'm sorry, Matt. I'm acting like a fool. It doesn't matter what happened back then. It was a long time ago."

"You're wrong about that. It does matter. It's why I came here. To tell you I was a jerk, and that it wasn't anything you did. It was me. I hated my life and my father and I just needed to get out. The problem was...*you* made me want to stay, in a place that was pounding the life out of me."

The bitterness in his voice was almost palpable.

"I didn't know it was that bad," I replied.

"That's the kicker. It really wasn't. I was just young and stupid. I could have done better in school if I'd tried. I could've handled my father differently, but all I ever did was challenge him, which only provoked him more, and then I just had to leave. I was always so angry." He reached across the seat and surprised me by taking hold of my hand. "But I shouldn't have left without saying goodbye to you. I should have kept in touch. It's not that I didn't think about you. I did. I thought of you all the time."

"I thought of you, too."

A car sped by. Its noisy engine overpowered the crickets, then the red tail lights disappeared around the bend and it was quiet again.

"Sometimes," Matt said, looking down at their clasped hands, "I had dreams about you that were so real, I would wake up and think you were in bed beside me. For days I wouldn't be able to get you out of my head."

I felt dizzy, as if I were floating up the crest of a wave and plunging down into the trough.

He had missed me. He'd had dreams about me.

And he was sorry for leaving.

It was remarkable how that those two small words – *I'm sorry* – could cure so much hurt over something so insignificant. These were things that happened in high school when no one knew what they were doing half the time.

Not that I knew what I was doing now. Truth be told, I was more confused at twenty-one than I had ever been in high school, because I felt a greater pressure to settle upon one path for the rest of my life. I once felt as if the whole world was open to me, that there were hundreds of paths to choose from and I would always be free to explore as many as I wished.

Lately all I felt was constraint. Pressure to pick one path – the obvious one – and to pick it now and live with it forever.

I squeezed Matt's hand. "It's fine. All that matters is that you came back to tell me. I'm glad you did."

"So am I."

It was a strong hand wrapped around mine, warm and comforting, and it reminded me of those evenings on the beach when we were children.

"So what happens now?" I asked uncertainly, as I swallowed over the painful lump that was forming in my throat. "You found me and made amends. Will you go back to Chicago?"

I didn't want him to say yes. I wanted him to stay here.

Matt turned my hand over and stroked my palm with the pad of his thumb. It made the stubborn lump in my throat grow even bigger.

"I guess so," he replied. "Now that I've seen you and apologized, I can tick this off my long list of regrets and move on to the next one."

"I hope it's not too long of a list." I tried to sound lighthearted, though inside I felt nothing of the sort.

"It's getting shorter," he told me. "I've dealt with a few things already – like the stuff with my dad. We talked, and it's better now. But what happened between you and me, the way I left without saying goodbye...I needed to make it right."

I could not, for one second, deny that I was pleased he considered me an important part of his life. He was an important part of mine, too. In this moment, nothing else even seemed to exist.

We sat for a long time in the tranquil hush of the night.

"I should take you back." Matt reached for the keys and started the engine. "I don't want to get you into trouble."

He smiled at me, but his eyes were melancholy.

A short time later, he dropped me off at the door. "So this is it?" I asked, not yet ready to get out of the car. "I won't see you again before you go?"

He shifted uneasily. "Probably not."

I couldn't bear to think that he had come here only to say he was sorry, and we would never see each other again.

"Are you sure? If you're here for a week, we could do something together. I could take the bus to Boston. We could meet somewhere."

He stared out the front window. "I don't think that would be such a good idea."

"Because of Peter?" I quickly asked.

There was something strange and unreadable in his eyes. I wished I could understand it. "Yeah."

"He wouldn't mind," I assured him. "I'll tell him you're in town. He'll understand."

"It's not just that." Matt opened and closed his fist over the steering wheel.

"What is it, then? Do you have other people to see?"

I could feel him drifting away from me, into that distant, unreachable place, and I didn't understand why.

"No," he replied. "I just don't want to complicate your life."

"How would it complicate it? We're old friends and you're here for a visit. It seems very simple to me."

Still, he hesitated, and I realized I was pushing myself on him, begging and pleading for one more day of friendship and togetherness, when clearly he didn't want it.

"Oh, let's just forget it," I lightly said, wanting to sink through the vinyl seat cushions and disappear. "I have a busy week anyway." I reached for the door handle. "But I'm so glad you came to see me, Matt. I had a nice time tonight, and if you ever come home to Camden, please look us up."

I was about to get out of the car when he grabbed hold of my wrist. "*Wait.*"

I froze.

"When?" he asked. "When do you want to get together?"

For a few frantic seconds, I couldn't seem to get my lips to move, then at last they began to work.

"The day after tomorrow? I only have one class on Tuesdays. I can miss it."

"How about in the morning? I'll pick you up at ten."

I wondered if Peter might be hurt by this, but I didn't let it hold me back. "All right."

Matt let go of my arm, and I got out of the car. He was leaning over the seat I had just vacated, looking up at me from the dark interior, frowning. "I'll see you Tuesday then?"

I nodded and shut the car door. A second later, he drove off, and I knew – even after all they had shared that night – that he was still keeping his distance.

I wanted to know why.

The next morning, I slipped a coin into the slot on the pay-phone. It jangled down inside, then I dialed the number for the plant and sat down on the stool.

It rang three times before Mrs. Weatherbee picked up at the other end. "Wentworth Industries."

"Hi, Mrs. Weatherbee. This is Cora. Can I speak to Peter?"

Her voice warmed instantly. "Oh, hello dear. How are you? How is school?"

"It's wonderful, thank you. Is your mother doing okay?"

"Yes, she's much better. The doctor gave her some pills and they've helped. Say hello to your mother for me, will you?"

"I will."

"I'll put you through now."

There was an audible *click*, then Peter picked up.

"This is Peter."

"Hi, it's me." I shifted uneasily on the hard stool.

He paused. "Why are you calling me in the middle of the day? Is something wrong?"

I tried to keep my voice light and cheerful. "No, nothing. I just wanted to call and tell you who I saw yesterday."

"Yeah? Who?" He sounded distracted, then I heard the buttons clicking on his adding machine.

"Matt."

The buttons stopped clicking. "You're kidding me."

I hadn't known what to expect, and was relieved that he didn't sound angry or concerned, but merely surprised.

I began to pick at a yellow sticker of the sun on the payphone, which was already half torn away. "No. I'm not. He showed up at the dorm. He's in Boston visiting his brother and stopped in to say hi."

The adding machine buttons started clicking again, and I heard the crank roll the tape. "So what did he say? How's he doing?"

I told Peter about Matt's job in construction and the fact that he had patched things up with his father.

"I never thought we'd ever hear from him again," Peter said.

"Neither did I. I was really surprised to see him."

I continued to pick at the yellow sticker, trying to slide my thumbnail under the glue to peel away the rest, but it wouldn't budge. I had to scrape at it.

"So when is he going home?" Peter asked.

"In a week."

He was quiet for a second. "Are you going to see him again?"

I pinched the bridge of my nose, knowing this was why I had called — to tell Peter exactly what was happening, so I wouldn't feel as if I were sneaking around on him. But the words seemed to lodge in my throat.

"Yes, I think so," I said at last.

There was nothing but silence on the other end of the line. No buttons clicking. No crank to roll the tape.

"Are you sure that's a good idea?"

"Why wouldn't it be?"

I could just see his face. He was probably shaking his head at me.

"Because it's Matt. Come on, you know what he's like."

For a number of seconds, I didn't speak because I wasn't sure what I was feeling. Part of me felt guilty for wanting to see Matt again. Peter would be very hurt if he knew just how badly I needed to.

Another part of me was annoyed at him for doing what he always did. He was holding me back, talking sense to me, as if I were a child who needed to be sheltered and protected.

Sometimes he was just too sensible. And to suggest that Matt was not worth my time for whatever reason made me want to scream. Yes, he had a history of being reckless and wild – unreliable, too – but he was still Matt, our childhood friend, and he'd matured and admitted he'd made mistakes. I couldn't just cut him off.

I suppose I still harbored some resentment toward Peter over the way our trio broke apart all those years ago, when I had wanted to at least try and hold it together. Peter had discouraged me. He had told me it was hopeless.

I looked up at what was left of the torn yellow sticker and spoke in a firm but reassuring voice. "It's no big deal, okay? He's just in town for a week. He's not going to corrupt me."

I didn't know where that had come from.

He let out a brisk huff. "I just don't think it's a good idea. I wouldn't trust him, Cora."

I clenched my jaw. "Look, you don't have to worry about me. I'm a big girl."

He was quiet on the other end.

"And maybe he's not like he used to be," I argued. "Maybe he deserves a second chance. Maybe he wants to make his life better, and if he does, I think we should be there for him. Not just me, Peter. You, too. Try to remember the good times we used to have – the snow forts and swimming in the summer. And you know how rough he had it with his dad. He didn't have a mother. It wasn't his fault he got so messed up."

I hadn't meant to say all that. I'd only meant to tell him I was going to spend a few more hours with Matt.

Nevertheless, I continued in a calmer voice. "I just think that we should forgive certain things. He really seems like he has some regrets."

I waited for Peter to respond.

"Regrets," he repeated. "Did he actually say that?"

"Yes. He said he knew Doug Jones and his buddy were idiots…And like I said, he's patched things up with his dad."

I heard Peter sigh deeply into the phone. "Why didn't he come back here to Camden? What was he doing at Wellesley?"

"He's visiting his brother in Boston," I told him again.

After a long pause, Peter said, "Well, I guess it's okay for you to go. Tell him I said hi, will you?"

9"And tell him to come home this winter when the lake's frozen," Peter added. "We could take our sticks out and shoot the puck around."

I tried to smile but couldn't seem to muster it. "I'll tell him, and maybe he will."

We talked for another few minutes about unrelated things, then said goodbye.

I hung up the phone with a tremendous sense of relief, because I'd done the correct and responsible thing. I'd told Peter my plans, and I'd also stood my ground and hadn't let him talk me out of doing what I wanted.

Why then, I wondered as I returned to my room and shut the door behind me, did I feel as if I were about to step off the edge of a very steep cliff?

Thirty-six

W hen Matt arrived to pick me up at ten o'clock the following Tuesday, I had no way of knowing that I would
later look back on that day as the great divider of my
life, for it was the day I would finally begin to believe in heaven.

That treasured morning dawned like a blue topaz – clear,
pure, and dazzling. I woke to piercing rays of sunshine stream-
ing in through the window. Birds chirped in the treetops; dew
gleamed on the grass. It was exactly the sort of day that promised
excitement and new discoveries.

Matt arrived perfectly on time, and I got into his car with a
curious smile. "So what are we doing today?" I set my bag on the
floor at my feet. "You told me to wear trousers and bring a warm
jacket. Let me guess. Are we going sailing?"

He squinted in my direction, taking his eyes off the road only
briefly. "You guessed it."

"On your brother's boat?"

"Right again."

I felt a jolt of excitement. "Is he coming, too?"

"No, he's at work today. It'll just be the two of us."

I looked out at the trees passing by the open window, the
branches blowing in the wind. "It's been a while since I've been
out on the water. I hope I don't sink us."

"Do you remember how to tie a bowline knot?" he asked.

"I think so."

"A reef knot?"

"Uh huh."

"And port is *which* side?"

"The left." I began to laugh.

He picked up speed once we were on the main road. "And what will you do if I yell *ready to tack*?"

"I'll duck out of the way of the boom."

He smiled. "I think we'll do just fine."

It was an unseasonably warm autumn morning, and for the first few miles outside of Wellesley, we drove with the windows down. We talked about our families, in particular Matt's brother, Gordon, who was a stockbroker, and his wife, *Rita*, a schoolteacher. I had heard that Gordon married a girl from Boston the previous year, but as far as I knew, he had never brought Rita home to Camden. Matt told me they were expecting their first child in January.

Feeling free and relaxed, I stuck my hand out the window and felt the force of the wind pushing against my open palm. I looked forward to feeling the wind on my face when we reached Marblehead and got under way.

The trip passed quickly. Soon we were driving through the historic town, past Our Lady Star of the Sea Church, and turning right toward the Boston Yacht Club on the harbor.

We took a launch out to the sloop, *Rita*, named for Gordon's better half, which was tied to its mooring. Matt climbed aboard, then offered his hand to me. I stepped over the weather rails onto the gleaming wooden deck.

"She's beautiful." I looked around the cockpit at the shiny brass steering wheel and all the freshly varnished maple. My gaze traveled up the tall wooden mast. Seagulls circled overhead against the blue sky, coasting on the wind, calling out to each other. A ship's bell rang somewhere nearby.

"Yeah, I wish she were mine," Matt replied, as he moved behind me toward the cabin hatch.

I felt the moist heat of his breath in my ear as he spoke, and my skin erupted in gooseflesh. Somewhat flustered, I watched him unlock and open the hatch.

"You can put your things down here." He climbed down the companionway to the darker confines below. "I brought sandwiches for later."

I followed him down and set my bag on the leather seat cushion along the port side of the cozy cabin, which was paneled in maple and smelled of lemon oil. There was a sturdy table and galley stove, and a private forward berth built for two.

"It's a beautiful boat. Have you sailed her much?"

"We took her to Virginia last year," he replied. "Just Gordon and me, the month before his wedding."

"His last hurrah?"

"I guess you could call it that, though I think he's happier now than he's ever been. Rita was the best thing that ever happened to him."

"That's nice to hear."

He stood before me, so dark and handsome in the dim cabin light, and I grew painfully aware of my heart beating like a drum. Then suddenly Peter's face flashed through my mind, and I felt a tremor of guilt.

"Ready to set sail?" Matt asked.

The boat moved upon the waves slapping against the dock. "*Rita* seems eager."

I steadied myself and tried not to complicate things by thinking of Peter. I had told him about this. I was doing nothing wrong.

"Let's get up on deck then," Matt said. "The wind is just right. We shouldn't waste it."

I followed him up the companionway ladder, and together we set about rigging the boat – unfurling the mainsail, inserting the battens, attaching the halyard. Matt raised the heavy mainsail himself, using all his strength to pull on the rope, hand over hand, the muscles in his arms and shoulders straining with every movement. The wind snapped the canvas like a flag as it lifted.

I stood by to tie it off, then together we prepared and raised the jib sheet.

At last, Matt took the helm. I untied the mooring line and we began to move.

CHAPTER

Thirty-seven

⸎⟶

"Where are we headed today, skipper?" I asked, hopping down into the cockpit to stand beside him.

He pointed toward open water. "That way, in the general direction of bliss."

I threw my head back and laughed. "Is that just west of Contentment Island?"

"So you've been there." He smiled back at me.

"No, but I've heard of it."

I laid a hand on his shoulder to keep my balance as the boat heeled to windward. We picked up speed. The sheets were tight, perfectly trimmed for the edge of the wind. The prow sliced through the frothy blue water, which swished past the hull.

Oh, how I gloried in the sensation of the wind and spray on my cheeks. I breathed in the salty, fresh fragrance of the sea, listened to the sound of the seabirds screeching overhead, following us out of the harbor. I felt exhilarated, euphoric.

"You're right," I shouted over the wind. "*This is bliss!*"

We were on a starboard tack, close-hauled, then Matt suggested a faster reach. I hopped up onto the foredeck and re-trimmed the sails. He turned the wheel for a beam reach, and we cruised faster, thundering and thrashing over the whitecaps, sharing in the excitement of our speed until it was time to turn.

"Ready to tack?" Matt called out. "You remember what to do?"

The wind whipped my hair wildly about my face. "Yes! Anytime you're ready!"

He nodded at me, then turned the wheel hard over and ducked. The boom swung across. I released the jib sheet for the new direction.

Switching sides, I checked the sail and cleated the lines.

"Want to take the helm?" Matt asked.

I hopped back down into the cockpit. "I'd love to."

Taking hold of the brass wheel and holding it steady, I watched Matt move to the bench and sit down.

He leaned forward and rested his elbows on his knees, clasped his hands together, lowered his head.

"Are you all right?" I asked.

He lifted his head. "Yeah, I just didn't sleep too well last night."

We continued to sail into the blue.

"You're quite a yachtswoman," he said. "You haven't lost your touch."

"It's like riding a bike I guess."

The rest of the world hardly existed for me in those moments as we coasted over the choppy waters. I was able to forget about my studies, my future, and even my name or where I came from. All that mattered was the speed and direction of the wind, and the pull of the boat's wheel in my hands.

And the fact that Matt was sitting beside me.

"This is amazing," I said.

I shaded my eyes to look out at the horizon, which rose and fell in the distance with the heaving motion of the boat. "She's an incredible vessel. She responds like a dream."

Matt was still sitting on the bench with his back to the transom, a knee raised, his arm resting over it. He was watching the horizon, too.

"I'm on cloud nine!" I shouted. "Thank you for taking me out here today. It's breathtaking. Honestly, it's like heaven!"

He stood up, sidled next to me and took hold of the wheel. We gripped it together for a moment, sharing the ecstasy of the day.

Then it was my turn to sit down and relax, so I let go of the wheel, plunked myself down on the bench and hugged my knees to my chest.

Matt's eyes were serene and riveting as he looked down at me. "So do you believe in heaven?" He grinned. "Since you mentioned it."

A lock of hair blew wildly across my face. I tucked it behind my ear. "I really don't know," I said. "Not that I don't think about it. I do. Quite a bit, actually, when I'm alone. The problem is, the rational part of my brain wants proof that it exists, but of course there isn't any."

The boat was leaning over, skimming across the clear water like a speed skater.

"But sometimes I think that maybe *this* is heaven," I continued, feeling Matt's attention turn curiously to my face, even though I was looking out across the distance.

"How so?"

"That it exists in these moments of pleasure," I tried to explain, "when a person is feeling completely fulfilled. You said we were headed for bliss today, and you were right. That's how I feel right now — surrounded by water and sky, breathing in the fresh, salty air. It's as if all my senses are alive. And isn't that what heaven is all about? The ultimate fulfillment? Isn't it supposed to be paradise?"

He squinted at me. "So you believe in heaven on earth."

I was not surprised by how easy it was to talk to him about something so profound. No one else in my life ever wanted to talk about these things. No one ever questioned it, at least not out loud, in conversation.

"Who knows?" I answered. "Maybe this is just a taste of what exists after death. Because all this joy – it's in our souls, isn't it? Not in our brains or the flesh of our bodies. Not even in our hearts. When people talk about the joy in a person's heart, what they really mean is the soul, don't you think? Because the heart is just an organ, and when we're gone, it stops. It dies with our bodies."

"But do our souls really go on?" he asked. "That's the real question."

I regarded him intently. "Do *you* think they do?"

The wind blew a part in his hair. He took his eyes off the horizon and continued to stare down at me. "I guess I'm looking for proof, too," he said, "just like you. Though some would argue that it's not proof we need, but faith."

He turned the wheel slightly to adjust to a shift in the wind, and I admired the clear, chiseled lines of his profile.

"Do you have it, Matt? Faith?"

"Sometimes," he replied, "on certain days. But maybe not enough. At least not yet. I guess I'm waiting for something – a bolt of lightning, a burning bush. I don't know."

"Mm," I agreed, chuckling softly. "Maybe these things become more clear as you get older."

"Maybe they do." He looked up at the large, white mainsail, straining against the wind. "But I do believe in everything else you said – that there can be heaven on earth in certain moments of our lives. This is one of those. I don't think it gets any better than this."

"Neither do I," I eagerly replied. "I hope my life will be full of moments just like this."

We smiled at each other, and something inside me trembled with a mixture of fear and yearning.

"Are you hungry?" Matt asked, changing the subject, lightening the mood. "We could head toward calmer waters and drop anchor."

"That sounds like a good idea."

It was mid-afternoon by the time we cruised into a quiet cove.

With great efficiency, we dropped the sails, lowered the anchor, then Matt went below and brought up a plate of sandwiches and a bottle of chilled white wine.

"You must miss this when you're in Chicago," I said, leaning back against the transom and watching his expression as he looked up at the sky.

I looked up, too – at a fluffy white cloud, drifting slowly by, over the tip of the mast.

"I go sailing on Lake Michigan sometimes," he said dropping his gaze and reaching for a sandwich. "But it's a strange experience."

"In what way?"

He took a bite and swallowed.

"Because it looks like the ocean and sounds like the ocean. Your eyes are telling you that's what it is, but there's something missing. Something…" He paused, as if searching for just the right word. "Something vital." He sipped his wine. "All of your senses become frustrated, because nothing smells quite right or tastes the way it should. It's a huge body of water, but it's fresh, so there's no salt on your lips or skin. There's an almost disturbing absence of smell once you get out far enough." He rested his arm along the back of the bench. "It's nice, but it's not the same as this."

"I never thought of that before," I said, though I was deeply aware of the sensuality of this day.

"I guess when you grow up by the sea," he said, "it's in your blood. You can never get away from it. It's a part of you."

"Doesn't that make you want to move home," I asked, "and spend your life on the coast?"

Lately I had been finding it difficult to imagine returning to Camden after graduation and settling down forever in my hometown. But if Matt was there, if I could see him every day, I couldn't imagine anything more perfect.

"Yes. Desperately."

Surprised by his answer, I frowned. "Then why don't you do it? Just pack up and come home."

He didn't respond at first. It was as if he wanted to ignore the question. Then after a while, he leaned back on an arm and looked down at the plate of sandwiches. "It's not that simple."

"Why?"

He gave me a long look and shook his head, telling me without words that he didn't want to talk about it.

I didn't push, despite the fact that I was burning with curiosity about his life in Chicago. What was keeping him there? It had to be something. Or some*one*. I felt a sudden stab of jealousy, imagining that there might be a woman in his life, even though he'd already told me there wasn't.

I told myself to be patient. There was time. He would reveal things when he was ready.

We finished eating the sandwiches and changed the subject to books. We talked about the novels we'd read over the years, and Matt opened up about the short stories he'd written and the novel he'd begun. He told me it was about a boy who had been orphaned and found an unlikely father figure in an old man who swept the streets of New York.

Again, I encouraged him to finish it.

"Maybe," he said. "We'll see."

The waves lapped up against the hull, and the seagulls circled over the boat. I couldn't remember the last time I had indulged myself in the magic of a day like this. The whole world seemed to be singing a rhapsody, vibrating with a special energy.

Oh, how I had missed Matt. I hadn't truly realized it until that moment. Over the past six years, I had blocked out the memory of the contentment I had known when we were together as children, because I was forever grieving the loss of it. It was as if, on the day Matt left Camden, half of my heart had been torn away.

With him, he had taken the part of me that could experience this sort of euphoria.

All at once, I wanted overwhelmingly to be closer to him, to slide across the bench and curl into his arms. I'd always wanted it, even when we were children, but I hadn't completely understood the foundation of those desires. I had not understood that my feelings, even then, were sexual.

There was no denying it now. Here I sat, stuck head-to-wind in this flashing moment in time. In one direction, there was safety on the shore – *Peter* – and in the other, there was Matt. He was the vast unknown with all its unpredictable dangers – the riptides and icebergs. Storms and breakers.

Matt gulped down the rest of his wine, then let the empty glass dangle from his fingertips as he looked out at the choppy Atlantic.

"Looks like there's a fog rolling in." He rose to his feet. "Do you see it?"

I stood up as well. "Yes. I can feel the chill."

"We should probably head back."

He faced me and reached out to take my empty wine glass. Our fingers touched briefly, and I felt it like an electric jolt through my body. I believe he felt it, too, because he stood there for the longest moment, staring into my eyes.

My lips parted. My heart began to race. I wanted to say something, but what? There were no words to describe what I felt or what I wanted. All I knew was that I was overcome by a desire so profound, no amount of self-discipline or control was powerful enough to stop it.

The boat lifted and I swayed toward him. It was all he needed. Matt stepped forward and pulled me into his arms. He held me close for a brief, tenuous moment while my heart beat wildly in my chest, then his mouth collided rashly with mine.

He tasted of freedom and ecstasy. My whole body quickened at the connection as his hands roamed over my hips and across my back, the lush heat of his mouth like a balm to my starving, raging senses. Disoriented and trembling, I wrapped my arms around his broad shoulders and held on tight, clutching at his jacket, wanting so much more than either of us had ever intended to take or give.

He bent his head and kissed the side of my neck until I was near to weeping with joy and misery, for I wanted him with a mad desperation.

"Oh, Matt," I sighed.

He tried to end it, to pull away, but couldn't. Instead, he held me close in his arms and touched his forehead to mine.

"God, Cora." The boat bobbed gently beneath our feet. "I should never have come here."

"Don't say that. I wanted this."

"But I promised myself I wouldn't touch you."

Frustration flooded through me, because I had been absolutely willing to dive into this headfirst, and was *still* willing. Consequences meant nothing to me now.

"Why?" I asked. "Because of Peter?"

"I told you before, I don't want to complicate your life. I'm not the one for you."

I sucked in a breath to speak, but he cut me off. "You know I'm not the type to stick around. I've never stayed with a job for more than a year. I can't finish a book I started five years ago. We both know what kind of person I am. I'm not steady, and you deserve better." He dropped his hands to his sides. "It's time to go back."

He turned to gather up the plates and the empty wine bottle, and just like that, the bond between us snapped. The passion in his eyes disappeared, smothered by what, I had no idea. Fear, perhaps. Concern for my welfare. Maybe even his loyalty to an old friend he hadn't seen in six years.

Or was it simply as he said – a natural inability to commit to anyone or anything? A deficiency that he would never overcome? Perhaps he didn't *want* to overcome it. Maybe he preferred his freedom. Maybe he would always grow bored with anything that became too familiar.

Maybe that was why I was so attracted to him. Because he was unattainable.

I couldn't speak. All I could do was move about methodically to help rig the boat.

Together, in silence, we drew up the anchor and hoisted the sails, and said very little to each other as the wind took us back to more familiar waters, and eventually back to dry land.

CHAPTER

Thirty-eight

❧

M att was distant during the sunset drive back to Wellesley
– so distant that he barely spoke to me. He kept his eyes
fixed on the road, and when we came to a set of lights
and had to stop, he reached across for a package of cigarettes in
the glove compartment.

He didn't look at me as he dug into his pocket for a pack of
matches, nor did he ask whether I minded if he smoked. He lit the
cigarette and dragged on it with relief – as if he'd been waiting all
day to do just that – then he shook the flame from the match and
dropped it into the ashtray.

He draped a wrist over the steering wheel and hung the other
arm out the window. "Come on, come on," he said impatiently
to the traffic light while the cigarette dangled from the corner of
his mouth.

It was the first time I had seen him smoke since he'd re-
entered my life. I had forgotten that he'd ever taken up the habit.

I rolled down my window. "So what are your plans for the
rest of the week?" I asked.

"Don't know."

He switched on the radio. The light turned green; he stepped
on the gas. We drove out of town, farther away from the sea until
I could no longer hear it or smell any trace of it.

I sat back in the seat and said nothing. He made no effort, either, to initiate any conversation.

A chill wind blew in through the open window. The scarlet light of the evening cast a queer glow on the trees at the side of the road. Matt turned the silver knob on the radio, pushed through noisy, obnoxious static, found music, and turned up the volume.

We drove for miles in silence. Eventually I just pretended to be asleep.

By the time we arrived back at Wellesley, it was full dark. Matt turned onto the campus. I reached over without asking and switched off the radio. It was quiet at last.

"Why don't you pull over right here," I brusquely said, feeling a powerful urge to hit something. "I can walk the rest of the way."

I didn't want him to drop me off at the main doors because I knew I would need time to wrestle with my mood before I faced anyone.

I also needed a few final minutes to chastise myself for becoming infatuated with Matt after a mere two days in his company. Hadn't I learned a long time ago that he was not capable of finishing what he began? It was why he left Camden. He could not manage the long haul of personal relationships or commitments. His personality could go from hot to cold in the space of a single heartbeat. He was fickle. When anything became too familiar, he was no longer interested.

What was I thinking, imagining that what I felt for him was more meaningful than what I had with Peter? Peter wanted to marry me. He wanted to commit to me for the rest of his life. He had been my constant, devoted friend since we were children. He had never strayed from that friendship, and my happiness and well-being meant everything to him.

He had even warned me about Matt. He'd wanted to protect me as he always did, because he loved me. He had been sensible and prudent, as always.

Matt pulled over under an oak tree. He did not turn off the car, which only fuelled the fires of my hostility. He made no mention of seeing me again, nor did he thank me for spending the day with him. He stared straight ahead, as if I had offended him in some way.

I suppose I had – for I allowed myself to adore him.

A single oak leaf floated down through the air like a feather onto the windshield.

I wrapped my hand around the door handle and thought about getting out with a mere, "See you around," but couldn't do it. It was not my way. Unlike Matt, I communicated my feelings, and I was going to be very frank.

"I don't know what's wrong with you," I said, "but you haven't spoken one word to me since we left Marblehead, and I want you to know how disappointed I am. I thought we had a nice time today, but now you've ruined it."

He finally looked at me.

"Did you think I was going to expect something from you?" I asked. "Is that what you're afraid of, that I might want a promise from you, or a marriage proposal? Have you been trying to tell me – in your own rude, cowardly way – that you're not interested? Well, you needn't worry, Matt, because I know you better than that. I know how quickly you get bored, how you hate to be boxed in. I know enough not to expect *anything* from you."

His Adam's apple bobbed as he swallowed. He said nothing for a few seconds, and when he spoke, his voice was quiet. "You should probably go."

He might as well have hit me in the face with a baseball bat.

Fighting tears, I picked up my bag, opened the door and got out. "You really are an ass, Matt. Do you know that? I never wanted to believe it before, even when Peter told me I couldn't trust you, but I guess I have no choice now. But I'm not letting you leave without telling you that you have broken my heart, because I never cared for anyone the way I cared for you. I thought we were the same, but now I have to accept that we're not. Because I'm not like you. I don't shut out the people I love."

I slammed the door and turned away, then let the tears gush from my eyes. Quickly, I made my way across the dark lawn in the direction of my dorm. I didn't allow myself to look back and see if he had driven away, even though, to my eternal chagrin, there was a part of me that hoped he would come running after me and tell me he was sorry, and plead with me to forgive him.

If Peter were here, he would tell me not to entertain such foolish hopes – that no, we could not be friends, because Matt could not be trusted. I was better off never seeing him again. For as long as I lived.

I stopped suddenly and wiped the exasperating tears from my cheeks. I could not walk into my dorm like this. I had to stop crying and catch my breath.

A car door slammed.

I turned around.

Matt was striding across the lawn toward me, with long, purposeful strides.

Oh, God...

My heart throbbed painfully in my chest. I couldn't breathe through my embarrassing shuddering sobs.

A part of me wondered if I should take off and run in the other direction. Then all at once he was upon me, backing me up against a tree, taking me into his arms and crushing his lips to mine.

I dropped my bag with a thud. My arms flew around his neck. It was like being swept out to sea. I couldn't find the resolve to kick against the current, because despite everything, I still wanted him with a passion that overcame reason.

I have no idea how long we stood up against that tree, kissing in the darkness while his hands explored my body, as if the world were coming to an end.

Finally he dragged his lips from mine. "*I'm so sorry.*"

Stunned and emotionally drained, I blinked up at him.

"I never should have come to see you," he said. "It was selfish. I shouldn't have taken you sailing today. I should have just left it."

"But why?"

He closed his eyes and shook his head.

Something was wrong. I could feel it. We had shared so much over the past few days. There had to be a reason why he pushed me away like this, and it was not what he had explained before.

"There's something you're not telling me," I said.

He grimaced, almost as if he were in physical pain.

"Tell me." I took his face in my hands.

"I'm sick," he finally confessed. "I have to have an operation in a couple of weeks, and if I don't have it, all the doctors tell me the same thing. That I won't live to see the spring."

I stood staring up at him, unable to move. "What kind of operation?"

"I have a tumor in my brain," he explained. "It has to be removed."

I felt like I was going to vomit. "Can they do that? Can they remove it and cure you?"

"I'm told there's a fifty-fifty chance."

"Fifty percent," I repeated in a daze, clinging to the hope that it would be successful. Of course it would. It *had* to be.

He stepped back, giving me a moment and some space to digest this. I moved away from the tree, wandering off a little ways to comprehend what he'd told me. I looked up at the dark, star-speckled sky.

"When did you find out?" I asked.

"A month ago. I was having headaches, so I went to see someone."

I turned to face him. "Do you still have them?"

"Yes. I have one now."

I wished I could take that pain away, but knew that I couldn't. I could do nothing to change what was happening. "Does your father know?"

"Yeah, but he's been keeping his distance. He hasn't called or anything since I told him."

I fought to contain my anger at the man who had abused Matt as a child, then drove him away from Camden, and who now could not bring himself to offer support when it was most needed. "I don't understand that," I said. "You're his son."

Matt merely shrugged. "I'm through with hating him. When something like this happens, you let go of all that stuff. I've forgiven him. That's all I can do. And I've told Gordon that. I'll want Dad to know it."

"Don't say things like that," I quickly said, almost scolding him with my tone. "You're going to be fine. Gordon won't have to tell him anything."

"I hope you're right."

A breeze whispered through the branches above us.

It would soon begin to rain. I could smell it in the air.

"Where will they do the operation?"

"In Chicago," he replied. "It's why I have to go back next week."

"Let me come with you," I said, wondering what Peter would say, but knowing that for once, it wouldn't matter.

"No," Matt firmly replied. "You don't have to do that."

I stepped closer. "I want to. I want to be there with you when you're in the hospital. And we could spend some time together between now and then."

He spoke harshly. "I said *no*, Cora. I don't *want* you there."

"Why? I'll give you space when you need it. I'll give you whatever you need. And what happens afterward, we can decide that later. I won't expect you to marry me or anything like that. Just let me spend the next few weeks with you. Just that. *Please*."

He gently touched my cheek, while I waited for his answer.

"I'm scared," I said.

His expression grew tender, then he took me into his arms again. Tears returned to my eyes, and I convulsed with weeping.

"Don't cry," he whispered, stroking my hair. "Please don't cry."

"Just let me come. Let me be with you."

The rain began to fall in a fine, silvery mist, cold upon my skin. Fog crept low along the ground.

Sophie

CHAPTER

Thirty-nine

I stood up at the kitchen table and shook my head at my mother. "I don't want to hear anymore. I can't."

"Yes, you can," she firmly replied, "and you will, because you *have* to hear it. You're not the only person in this world who has suffered, Sophie. Life is hard. It's cruel sometimes. It's merciless and unfair, but we all go through difficult times, one way or another. You've had more than your share of knocks lately, I'll give you that, but it doesn't mean you get to quit. No one gets to quit. You keep fighting, every day, and sooner or later, the grief fades a little. You grow stronger, find joy again, and everything gets easier. You come out of it more equipped to handle the next wave, which will come eventually. There will always be waves."

I heard what she was saying, but my mind was fixed on something else she had told me about that night on the lawn at Wellesley. *I'm scared*, she had said to Matt.

I sat back down. "Megan told me she was scared. When she was in the hospital, in those last few days…She said she was afraid of dying."

My mother inclined her head at me. "And what did you tell her?"

"I told her that there were kind and beautiful angels waiting for her in heaven, and that they would love her and take good care of her." I swallowed over the jagged stone of despair in my throat. "But then she asked if I would be there, too, and I had to tell her no, I couldn't go with her. That she had to go alone." My throat was closing up. I barely managed to get the words out before my voice broke. "And she said, '*But I want my mommy.*'"

I covered my face with both hands.

I had not told anyone about that conversation, not even Michael. I had never been able to repeat it aloud. I could not even bear to think of it.

"You said the right thing, Sophie."

"Did I?"

Oh, God....

"Yes, you were a wonderful mother. No one will ever be able to take that away. Not from you or her. Megan had a beautiful life with you. She was loved more than any child could ever dream of being loved."

The tears in my eyes blurred my vision, and I struggled to blink them away.

My mother stood up and fetched a tissue from the box by the telephone. She handed it to me, and I wiped the tears from my cheeks.

"Did he have the operation?" I asked, wetting my lips, reclaiming the steadiness of my voice. "Did you go back to Chicago with him? Did he let you stay?"

"Yes." She sat back down.

"What happened?" I was desperate to know the answer. "Was it a success? Did he live?"

My mother turned her gaze toward the window and took a deep breath before she told me the rest.

Mountains

CHAPTER

Forty

༺☙༻

Cora

After Matt told me a bit more about the operation, I went back to my dorm room when all I wanted to do was stay with him, to get back into his car and drive far away for hours and hours. Tearing myself away from him was – up until then – the most difficult thing I had ever done.

I didn't sleep a wink. I tossed and turned and cried. Eventually I got up and sat in the window. When the sun finally appeared over the horizon, I waited until a reasonable hour, then called Matt at his brother's place and asked him to come and get me right away.

He said no. He told me to go to all my classes, and that he would meet me outside afterward. That was the condition. He didn't want to be responsible for me flunking out of Wellesley.

We went out for dinner again that night, and walked around town holding hands, talking about anything and everything. Not just his illness. Good things, too, like the book he had been working on.

The leaves were changing, but the air was balmy. We walked for a long time, sat under a tree for a while, and I was never so content or so grateful just to be alive and in his presence. Despite the terrible news he had delivered the night before, I felt extremely fortunate to be spending those hours with him. Everything was magical – the smell of the autumn leaves in the air, the sound of his voice, the familiar scent of his skin.

I knew, as the night wore on, that Matt was my true soul mate, and that nothing I'd ever experienced with Peter could compare.

Don't misunderstand me. I loved Peter deeply and felt guilty for this betrayal, but what Peter and I shared was different from this. Our relationship was practical and sensible. We were best friends, and I respected him. He was decent and honest and had been raised in a good family. My own parents adored him – they never cared much for Matt – but none of those things mattered as much to me as the harmony I experienced with Matt. Whenever we were together, all was right with the world, and I knew I was going to have to confess this to Peter and my parents.

Oh, how I dreaded the thought of it.

⸺❧⸺

I didn't wait or put it off. I felt it was important to do the right thing. It's what Peter would have expected of me, and I of him if the situation were reversed.

So, again, I slipped a coin into the slot on the payphone, sat down on the stool, and with a heavy lump in my stomach, listened to the coin fall inside.

A moment later, Peter picked up on the other end of the line.

"Hi Cora," he said. "I hope this is important because I'm really busy. I can't get this balance sheet to balance."

I swallowed uneasily and considered doing this another time...

When I didn't' speak, and the seconds ticked by like minutes, Peter asked, "Is everything okay?"

Struggling to steady my nerves, I sat up straight on the stool. Heartache throbbed inside my chest.

"Not really," I replied. "I have some bad news. It's about Matt."

Another awkward silence rolled through the telephone wire and filled my heart with dread.

"Well…" I didn't know where to begin. "He's not doing so well. He's sick, Peter. He has…" I paused. "He has brain cancer."

Just saying the words out loud caused a hot ball of fire to ignite in my gut. I took a deep breath and forced myself to continue. I couldn't fall apart.

"My God," he said. Neither of us spoke for a few seconds. "Is he going to be okay? Can they do anything for him?"

"They're going to operate to try and remove the tumor," I explained. "He told me there's a fifty percent success rate if he survives the surgery. He's young and healthy, so that's a good thing."

"Fifty percent. Those aren't great odds, Cora."

My stomach churned and I shut my eyes. "That's not what I want to hear right now," I said. "It's not helpful. And besides, I disagree. I think they're excellent odds. We need to stay positive and hope for the best. Promise me you'll do that."

He was quiet for a minute. "I just think we should prepare ourselves, that's all. I'd hate to see you get your hopes up."

God! I was so angry with him in that moment! I wanted to shout into the phone, reach through the wires and shake him. He was always so cautious about everything. I'm sure if it was up to him, he'd tell Matt to go check himself into the hospital right now because there was no point in doing anything else. And while he was there, he should write his obituary so it would be ready to go into the morning paper after the operation. Just in case.

"Well, I am going to get my hopes up," I told him, "and that's where they're going to stay. I'm going to talk to Matt about the future and how great his life is going to be when he gets out of the hospital. I'm going to spend every minute with him and make plans for next year, and the year after that."

Another pause. "What kind of plans?" Peter asked.

I looked up at the ceiling as a wave of sadness washed over me. How was I supposed to say this over the phone? How could I tell Peter how I truly felt? He was going to be crushed.

"I don't know, exactly," I replied. Not because I was trying to spare his feelings, but because it was the truth. Matt had never been the sort of person to stay in one place for very long. He was a wanderer – or at least he had been up until this point in his life. With or without the surgery, I knew the future would be uncertain. I couldn't be sure that he would give me his whole heart forever or get down on one knee and propose.

But did I even want that? Wasn't that part of the problem in my relationship with Peter? He was ready to say *I do*, while I was having doubts and feeling as if I was suffocating.

Knowing, however, that Peter deserved a better answer than the one I had just given, I cleared my throat and continued. "I don't know what the future holds, but I can't lie to you. I have feelings for Matt. I've always had feelings for him and I need to be with him right now."

I heard the chair creak in his office, then he got up and closed the door.

"I don't understand. What are you saying?"

I took another deep breath. "I'm saying that I need my freedom so that I can spend time with him."

He scoffed. "Is this what I think it is? We're breaking up? Is that what this phone call is really about?"

"I'm so sorry."

"Sorry?" His anger made me jump. "Have you lost your mind? You've spent two days with this guy and all of a sudden you want to throw away something we've had since we were kids? We're supposed to get married. We've been in a relationship for almost five years. I think you better put some more thought into this, Cora. He's not reliable, and besides, he could be dead in a month."

"*Peter!*" I couldn't listen to those words. I knew he was hurt and angry, but that was crossing the line.

And I most certainly had put thought into this. I had thought about it my entire life. Even while we were apart, Matt was always there, living in my heart. I had missed him and longed for him, and it didn't matter how much time we had left. Even if it was going to be brief, I had to take it.

I hoped, of course, that it would not be brief. I wanted to be with Matt until I drew my last breath.

The surgery was going to be a success. That's what I told myself over and over, and when he recovered, everything was going to be different. We were going to make up for lost time.

Peter was wrong about Matt. In every possible way.

Forty-one

⸙

The phone call with Peter did not end well. He wanted to know how much time I had spent with Matt, and if we had kissed or "done anything."

I told him the truth, that yes, we had kissed and held hands.

Peter didn't say anything right away, but I heard the stress in his breathing. Then he told me he never wanted to see my face or hear my voice again. He hung up without saying good-bye.

I went back to my room and cried for a while, and wondered if he was right. Maybe I had lost my mind. I remembered how Matt had treated me in the car on the way back from Marblehead, when he had shut me out with such ice-cold derision.

Peter had never treated me that way. We had never hurt each other, nor had we ever argued heatedly about anything. At least not until today.

A short while later, I dragged myself up off the bed and returned to the phone booth to drop another coin into the slot. This time I would tell my parents about Matt's illness and explain how I had just broken Peter's heart and ended our unofficial engagement. I suspected they weren't going to be happy about it either. And I was right. They were very sorry to hear about Matt's diagnosis, but they were deeply confused and bewildered by my decision to end things with Peter, for he had become an important part of our family. They adored him, and they were concerned for me.

⟿

Over the next five days, Matt and I spent every possible waking moment together. He wouldn't let me skip any classes, so he dropped me off five minutes before each class and was there outside the building waiting for me when I came out.

If I had assignments or papers to write, he took me to the library, sat next to me and worked on finishing his own book while I studied or researched.

I won't say it was easy. I had no interest in anthropology while he was sitting across a table from me, looking more handsome and appealing than any man had a right to be. He was quite a distraction, and if I wasn't simply marveling at how attractive he was, I was worrying about that tumor in his brain and dreading the operation and everything he would have to endure before he recovered.

Or what if this was it? I wondered miserably. What if he didn't survive and these were our last days together?

Was he afraid? I was, but I couldn't let him know it. Whenever my thoughts ventured into those disturbing territories, I took hold of my heart with a firm hand and redirected my thinking. A simple smile from Matt was usually enough to calm me. That's when I realized I could hide nothing from him. Somehow he always sensed when I was afraid. His gaze would lift from the pages of his notebook. In those moments he would kiss my hand or my cheek, and reassure me without ever speaking a word.

We were connected to each other. We always would be. No matter what happened, I knew that nothing about our relationship would be brief.

⤚ⲟ

I dreamed, on the fifth night, that I was walking through the forest at dusk. An owl hooted somewhere nearby. A thick layer of amber-colored pine needles carpeted the ground, and I could feel them snap and break beneath my feet as I meandered through the trees. I could hear the whispery rush of the sea from somewhere beyond my little grove. I could smell the saltiness, feel the chill of a fog bank rolling in...

Everything was still all around me, and suddenly I grew frightened. I felt very alone.

Then I heard a terrible roar behind me and thought it was an animal. I whipped around just as a cold ocean wave crashed into me, lifted me off my feet and carried me out of the woods.

I'm not sure how the dream ended, but I think I must have drowned. I woke up in a panic, gasping for air.

⤚ⲟ

Matt picked me up at lunch hour the following day, and I told him about the dream.

As soon as I mentioned the wave that swept me away, he looked at me sharply and pulled over onto the side of the road.

He sat staring straight ahead, gripping the steering wheel, tapping his thumb on it. Then he slid across the seat and pulled me into his arms.

I had always known that Matt was a spiritual person, but on the surface he appeared tough and masculine to the rest of the world. In high school, because of the way he dressed and smoked and drank, most kids were afraid of him.

But when I told him about my dream, he broke down in front of me and wept into my arms like a child who had become lost and was just found.

I'm not sure how long we sat there in his brother's car, but I remember very clearly how I held him and kissed the top of his head and stroked his hair. No matter how tightly I held him, however, I couldn't seem to get close enough. I loved him with such passion. There are no words to describe it. I would have died for him that night, if it would have taken away his pain.

At the same time, I knew he wouldn't have let me because he would have done the same for me. It's why he was crying. He knew my dream was a product of my fear. He was facing death, and therefore, so was I. He was mourning the fact that I had to share his pain.

"I'm so sorry," he said. "I didn't want to take you with me into this. I should have stayed away."

"No," I told him. "It would have been worse if you'd stayed away, because my life would have been consumed by regret – the regret of not being with you. Thank God you came. Otherwise hell would have followed me forever."

That night, after dark, we found a deserted country road outside of town and parked for a while. We climbed into the back seat, kissed and took off some of our clothes so we could touch each other. He asked if I was still a virgin and I told him I was, but I didn't want to be. Not with him.

He insisted that we should wait, because the future was so uncertain.

I agreed, but very reluctantly, and only for the time being.

CHAPTER

Forty-two

ometimes life can be impossibly cruel. I know that now.
I discovered it in those days leading up to Matt's surgery,
when we didn't know if it was the beginning of our life
together or the end.

But that's life, isn't it? For all we know, each day could be our
last. What matters most is the appreciation and gratefulness we
should feel for each precious day we have with one another.

I lived more passionately in those five days with Matt than I'd
lived my entire life. His pain was my pain, but the corresponding
joy was immense. We were one, and that closeness, that connection, is what brought me closest to heaven.

Love is our greatest achievement. Don't ever forget that.
Don't squander it. Seek it. Experience it. Savor it every day that
you can, because you never know when a rogue wave might sweep
you away.

"What if I choose not to have the surgery?" Matt said to me one
afternoon while we were sitting by the lake on campus, watching
the rowers.

"What do you mean? You have to have it."

He leaned back on an elbow and looked out at the water. "No. The doctor gave me a choice. He said that if I have it, there's a fifty percent chance I'll die on the operating table. If I don't have it, I could live for a whole year."

"Six months to a year," I reminded him, because every minute counted.

He glanced across at me. "The surgery's in a week, which is making six months look pretty good right now, if I knew I could spend it with you."

"Of course you could spend it with me," I said. "I'm not going anywhere, no matter what happens, but I don't think that's the right choice. The surgery could cure you completely. We have to try."

He nodded and tossed a small pebble into the water. "I know. I just thought I'd mention it."

I inched closer to him and laid my arm across his hips. "I guess it is something to consider. But don't ask me to give up hope. Right now there's a good chance that in a month's time, that tumor could be gone and you could be making plans for the future."

He thought that for a moment. "If I do get my future back, I will do whatever it takes to get you to marry me."

I chuckled softly while a warm glow lit up my insides. "You wouldn't have to do anything too difficult. I'd marry you tomorrow if you asked."

He gave me a sexy look. "I thought you weren't ready to be Miss Suzie Homemaker."

"That was before. Things are different now."

Carefully, he studied my eyes. "Because I might die?"

"No," I firmly replied. "Because you're here. Everything was wrong when you were gone from my life. Now it feels right again."

He reclined onto his back and watched the clouds roll by. I, too, lay down and looked up at the sky.

"It does feel right," he said. "I don't ever want to be apart from you again, Cora. You're like…the other half of me."

"I don't want to be apart from you either, which is why I want you to have that operation."

He took hold of my hand and squeezed it. "Okay."

Then suddenly, he squeezed it so hard, I cried out in pain. I jolted upright, just as his whole body began to seize.

"Matt! Are you all right?"

But he couldn't answer me. His eyes were rolling back in his head as he convulsed. I screamed for help, and people came running.

⟵⟶

The seizure stopped before the ambulance arrived, but Matt didn't regain consciousness until he reached the ER.

He was admitted and kept overnight while the doctors communicated with the medical team in Chicago to determine whether or not he should be released. There was some talk of airlifting him back and doing the surgery right away, but the following morning, when his vitals improved, they told us he could go home, but that he shouldn't get behind the wheel of a car because there was a high likelihood of more seizures, which could occur at any time without warning.

Matt's brother, Gordon, who had come to the hospital that morning, gave me the keys to the car and told me to do the driving from that moment on.

I went to see my professors in the afternoon, explained my situation, and told them I would be gone for a few weeks. They

were exceedingly helpful and gave me advance reading assignments and papers to complete while I was gone, and told me to
come back when I was ready.

Matt and I left for Chicago the following day.

I didn't tell my parents.

That night, we checked into a roadside motel, and I wondered
what my parents would think if they knew where I was or that I
was about to share a bed with Matt, after breaking up with Peter
only a week ago. To me, it felt like a lifetime.

I knew I would have to confess eventually. I just wasn't ready
to talk about it yet, or defend my decision to put everything aside
for him. They simply wouldn't understand. No one would.

Matt carried our bags in and set them down at the foot of
the bed.

"I wonder if this is some kind of test." He shrugged out of his
leather jacket and tossed it onto the chair. "I've worked hard to be
a gentleman so far, and God knows you deserve nothing less, but
I can't sleep on the floor tonight, Cora. I want to be close to you."

Immediately, I wrapped my arms around his neck. "That's
what I want, too. No one knows we're here. It's just us. You and
me. As far as I'm concerned, the rest of the world doesn't even
exist, so we can live by our own rules."

He held me tight, then pressed his lips to mine. I felt like a
woman, not a girl anymore. He was my mate, my partner, my
great love, and nothing had ever felt so right and so real. I had
no doubts about anything, and as I unbuttoned his shirt and slid
my hands across his warm, muscular chest, all I wanted to do was
give everything to him and take everything I could in return.

Our passions escalated quickly. Within seconds, I was kicking off my shoes and pulling my sweater off over my head.

Matt ripped his shirt off and eased me down onto the bed. His body covered mine in a wild frenzy of desperation. He kissed me fiercely and thrust his hips forward, cupping my behind in his hands and pulling me closer, almost roughly, but never hurting me.

We still wore our jeans, which was the only thing stopping us from making love. He unhooked my bra and caressed my breasts, kissed my neck tenderly, told me he loved me.

"I love you, too," I whispered. "I'll love you forever."

Everything about him aroused me. I wanted him with a fire that defied reason.

I had never been able to give myself to Peter. This was why. Matt was the one, and nothing could have held me back from this. Nothing else mattered. I didn't care how much time we had together. All I cared about was this moment in his arms, our bodies pressed together in love. I wanted to give him everything.

He unbuttoned my jeans and slid his hand down inside, and I climaxed almost immediately.

His open mouth smothered my cries, as I fumbled with his belt and tried to push his jeans down over his hips.

"No," he whispered into my mouth, shaking his head and eventually rising up onto his hands and knees. "I don't want to do this, not yet. I want to marry you."

I blinked up at him in a bewildered haze of arousal and confusion. "I don't care about that. Please, I want to be as close to you as possible. Tonight."

Brow furrowed, he stared down at me. "I can't do that. We need to wait. I don't know what's going to happen."

Cradling the back of his head in my hand, I pulled him close for another soul-reaching kiss. "I don't know either, which is why

I want to make the most of every minute. Please make love to me. I want you to be the one."

My heart was pounding like a hammer. All my nerve endings quivered with a feverish need to give everything to him, but in the end, he would not give himself to me in return.

A heavy tear fell from his cheek to mine, and he sat up on the bed, raked his fingers through his hair, and shook his head. "I can't. Not until I know for sure that I'll be around to be with you forever."

I sat up too, wrapped my arms around his neck, and told him that I loved him.

But I wanted more. I wanted so much more.

CHAPTER

Forty-three

I rose from the bed, opened my suitcase, and went into the bathroom to change into my nightgown and brush my teeth. While the water poured in a hissing rush out of the faucet, I sat on the edge of the tub and quietly wept. They were not tears of misery, however. I was expressing a strange mixture of emotion – something I had never experienced before – a simultaneous mingling of rapture and sorrow.

On one hand, I was afraid for the future. On the other, I was euphoric. I loved Matt with every fiber of my being, and I knew that he loved me, too. It was the most beautiful thing I had ever known.

A short while later, I returned to bed and watched him go into the bathroom. He closed the door behind him.

I lay quietly, listening to the shower.

Sometime before dawn, Matt rolled on top of me and kissed my neck.

"I love you," he whispered, and I immediately wrapped my legs around his hips and pulled him tight against me.

I could feel his arousal through the thin fabric of my nightgown, which was now bunched around my hips.

Again, he stopped and pressed his forehead to mine, shut his eyes and shook his head. "This is difficult."

"It doesn't have to be," I replied. "Let me ask you this…If I wasn't a virgin – if Peter and I had made love – would you make love to me now?"

"Yes."

I sucked in a breath. "Then please…It doesn't matter what I've done, or haven't done, in the past. I want you to be the one, no matter what happens. I know the risks. Please, don't deny me this. If you do, I'll never forgive you. I'll regret it for the rest of my life."

"Me, too."

While he spoke the words, his hand was already sliding up my thigh, pushing my nightgown out of the way.

Quickly, before he changed his mind, I shoved his pajama pants down over his hips and thrust my pelvis forward.

It was all very natural and easy after that. There was some pain, of course, but I welcomed it. I was so happy that night, I can't possibly express it. He made love to me slowly and gently and it was the most amazing experience of my life. It was every-thing I imagined it would be.

I loved him so much.

I will never regret it.

Forty-four

❧

Matt and I stayed in his Chicago apartment for three days before the date of his surgery.

I won't describe those days, except to say that we enjoyed each other immensely and made the most of every moment. We laughed and cried, watched television and played cards. We went out to eat and ordered in.

He showed me the box of manuscripts he had hidden away in his closet. I read his short stories and the novel he had finally finished. I made him promise to submit it to a publisher when he recovered, because I was quite certain it was the greatest novel of all time, though I admit that I may have been biased. Everything about Matt was perfect in my eyes. To me, he was a work of art, but I suppose that's how love feels.

I called my parents as well, and told them everything.

Well, almost everything. There are certain things you just don't share with your mother.

I let them know that Matt would have the tumor removed on November 17 at 6pm.

My mother then told me that Peter had come to the house to ask about me. He was very angry. They couldn't blame him, and they did their best to talk him through his pain.

I apologized to my parents, but told them it could be no other way, because Matt was the one I loved.

In the end, they wished me well and promised to pray for him.

—⟲—

On Sunday night, Matt was admitted to the hospital so they could run tests and prepare him for the surgery, which would last approximately six hours.

On Monday morning, a nurse shaved his head. He couldn't eat or drink all day, and he had to have X-rays and blood work.

Gordon arrived around noon and told us he would stay in Chicago as long as we needed him while Matt recovered.

Their father called shortly after Gordon arrived and spoke to Matt for a few minutes. He wished him luck and promised to visit him the next day.

Privately, I thought of their mother and wished she were alive to be here with us at Matt's bedside, but she had been gone a long time.

Matt mentioned her when he hung up the phone. He looked at Gordon and said, "I really miss Mom."

Gordon nodded and said, "I'm sure she's here."

We all sat very quietly.

—⟲—

Later, I flipped through the pages of a magazine while the nurses puttered about. It was all an act of course – the way I sat so casually. I had no interest in the magazine. My brain was on high alert, listening to everything, watching everything. My heart was burning with terror and dread. I couldn't eat or drink either.

Why was this happening? I wondered bitterly. All I wanted was for Matt to be healthy, to come out of the surgery with a positive prognosis. I wanted to spend the rest of my life with him. I would have sacrificed everything – my family, my education – in exchange for the success of that operation.

It was not up to me, however.

I knew it, even then.

Fate had its own designs, and part of that design was about to knock me flat on my back. An hour before Matt was scheduled for the OR, the most unexpected thing happened.

I look back on it now with gratitude. At the time, however, I was concerned.

ensing that Gordon needed some time alone with Matt, I
rose from my chair and offered to get us each a cup of coffee.
A moment later, purse in hand, I went to the elevator and
pressed the button. As the doors slid open in front of me, I took
a step back, for I found myself staring into the eyes of the man I
had just jilted.

Peter frowned at me. I suppose he was shocked to find me
standing there, as if I'd known he was coming.

What was he doing here? I wondered. Had he come to talk
me out of ending our relationship? To win me back?

Or had he come to confront Matt about stealing me away?

Rage pounded through me. I had only one hour left with
Matt before he would be taken to the OR, and I wasn't about to
let Peter take that precious time away. Whatever he wanted, it
would have to wait.

The doors started to close, and we both realized that neither
of us had moved or spoken. Quickly, he hopped off and shoved
his hands into his jacket pockets, glancing over his shoulder with
a mild look of irritation.

"Peter, if you've come here to fight with me or challenge
Matt, now's not the time," I said. "They're taking him to surgery
in an hour."

"I know." He looked down at the floor and shook his head. "That's not why I'm here."

My anger subsided as I watched him shift his weight uneasily from one foot to the other.

"Then why are you here?" I asked.

His eyes lifted, and I realized that what I had first perceived as anger was something else entirely. It was concern.

"I thought you could use a friend today," he said.

The whole world disappeared for a moment, then I could do nothing but step into his arms and hold him close.

"I don't want to cause any trouble," Peter said, as I wiped the tears from my cheeks. "But I'd like to see Matt if that's okay. It's been a long time."

"Of course," I replied. "He's just down the hall." All thoughts of coffee left my mind as we walked together to Matt's room. "Don't be too surprised when you see him. He's lost a bit of weight and the nurses shaved his head this morning. He won't look like the Matt you remember."

"It doesn't matter. I just want to wish him luck." We stopped outside the door and Peter turned to me. "Maybe later you and I can talk about some things."

"Of course."

I knocked on Matt's open door and entered, then gestured toward Peter, who walked in behind me. "Look who's here," I said, laboring to sound cheerful.

Matt took one look at Peter, and his eyes glistened with wetness. He struggled to sit up. "My God. Look at you. Come on in."

Peter approached the bed and bent forward to hug Matt. I had to fight against another powerful onslaught of tears.

"You're not here to punch my lights out I hope," Matt joked. "It wouldn't be too difficult, under the circumstances."

We all laughed awkwardly. It wasn't an easy situation.

"No, I came to wish you luck. It's going to be a long surgery, I hear."

Matt filled the awkward silence with an explanation about how they were going to drill into his skull, remove the tumor, and put everything back together afterward. He described some of the risks , then asked about Pete's family, and how work was going at the pulp and paper plant.

When another strained lull in the conversation arose, Matt looked at me. "Cora, would you give Peter and me a minute? I need to say a few things."

"Of course." But I couldn't seem to move my feet.

Gordon was at my side instantly. "We'll go get that coffee now," he said, as he led me out of the room.

We didn't leave the floor, however. I, for one, wasn't about to spend ten minutes lined up in the cafeteria. Gordon felt the same. All we did was stroll up and down the wide corridor, waiting for a reasonable amount of time to pass before we could return.

I wondered what Matt was saying to Peter, and suspected he was apologizing for stealing me away, and for deserting us in high school when he became friends with Doug Jones.

I had not forgotten the list of regrets Matt had told me about the first time he came to see me at Wellesley, and was quite sure he was ticking this one off, too.

He was making things right.

Peter left Matt's room a few minutes later and found us by the nurses' station. "Thank you," he said, "for letting me see him. I'd like to stick around if you don't mind. I'm going to grab some coffee now, but I'll find you in the waiting room later. He told me what floor he'd be on for the surgery. I'll sit with you, if you like?"

I touched his arm. "That would be nice."

I watched Peter get on the elevator, then hurried back to Matt's room.

Gordon didn't follow.

CHAPTER

Forty-six

❦

A nurse was taking Matt's blood pressure when I entered the room, so I waited quietly at his bedside, holding his hand. He looked at me with playful, sexy eyes, and we shared a private chuckle at the strangeness of all this. We were young, passionate lovers, but here we were, mucking our way through blood work, brain seizures, and the terrifying notion of dying early in life during a complicated and dangerous surgery, now only minutes away.

As soon as the nurse left the room, I lowered the bedrail and climbed onto the mattress next to him. He put his arm around me. I laid my head on his shoulder.

"It's going to be fine," he said. "Everything's going to be okay."

I touched his lips with the pad of my finger and said, "Of course it will, and I'm going to be right here when you wake up."

Leaning up on an elbow, he pressed his lips to mine and reminded me of how virile he was, despite these unthinkable circumstances. If not for the fact that a nurse could walk in at any moment, we would have made love, for we were both aroused. We understood the meaning of self-restraint, however, and laughed about the inconvenient IV line that was blocking our intentions, and the constant noise outside the door.

Eventually we gave up on the possibility of messing around like a couple of teenagers, and simply held each other.

"I'm glad you came to find me," I told him. "These past few weeks have been the happiest of my life." I rested my chin on his chest and looked up at him. "And all those years together in Camden...We were just kids, but it always felt like more. Now you're here with me again, and I don't ever want to be apart."

"We won't be. You've given me something to fight for, Cora. I want to be with you, so I'm going to make it through this, and tomorrow we'll start making plans."

I managed a pained smile and fought hard to believe him. I just had to. The alternative was unthinkable.

"I love you," he whispered, as he kissed my forehead and held me close. "I've said it before, but I need to say it again. I want to spend the rest of my life with you. *I want to marry you, Cora. I hope you'll say yes.*"

My eyes filled with tears. "Of course I will. I'm saying it right now. *Yes.*"

Just then, three nurses marched into the room. One of them started clapping her hands. "All right you two love birds. Break it up. This isn't a hotel room."

I laughed as I wiped a tear from my face, slid off the bed and rose to my feet.

"It's time to go now," another said. "We're going to wheel you to surgery and take very good care of you. I promise you that."

She met my gaze directly. "You can follow us and keep holding his hand until we reach the OR doors. Then you'll have to wait outside."

I took hold of Matt's hand and squeezed it. "I'll be there the whole time."

⟶ᴄ

Peter was sitting outside the OR in the waiting area, blowing on his hot coffee. I paused a moment to watch him – he hadn't noticed me yet – and wondered what I had done to deserve such kindness from him.

In my own mind, I had always denied him what he wanted most – my complete and utter devotion. Even my virginity I had given to Matt without hesitation after barely more than a week, and I wondered if Peter somehow knew it. Could he sense it, or see it in my eyes?

He looked up at that moment and smiled at me, and all my fears faded away. No, he didn't know how far Matt and I had gone. He was completely unaware.

"How are you doing?" he asked, when I sat down next to him.

"As well as can be expected." I checked my watch and counted forward six hours. "But I think it's going to be a very long night."

I was surprised when he touched my hand. "Yeah, but you'll get through it, Cora. He's going to be fine. You'll see."

I hoped so. I really hoped so.

Peter, Gordon and I sat together in silence for a long time. Peter read the newspaper while I tried to read a magazine, but eventually I tossed it aside because I couldn't concentrate on the pictures or words. All I could do was stare at the wall and wrestle with my fears, or think back on all the special moments Matt and I had spent together.

I thought about how blue his eyes were, and how I had become so lost in them, even as a young girl. I remembered kissing him for the first time on Gordon's sail boat, and I heard the sound of his voice in my ears. I want to marry you, Cora. I hope you'll say yes.

After a while, I stood up to stretch my legs and wandered around the waiting room, strolled a little way down the corridor, careful not to step on the lines between the tiles. It was a childish game, I knew, but I needed some sort of distraction.

It was quiet in that wing of the hospital, and I felt very alone. All I wanted was for Matt to push through those swinging doors at the end of the hall, walk toward me with a smile, and say that it was all over and everything was going to be fine.

I leaned against the wall and stared down at my feet.

"Are you okay? Can I get you anything?"

I lifted my gaze and realized Peter was standing in front of me. "No, thanks. I'm fine."

A voice came over the speaker system. "Your attention please. Visiting hours are now over. Visitors may return tomorrow morning at 10:00 a.m."

"I don't think that's for us," Peter said, leaning a shoulder against the wall. "We're okay here."

I nodded.

Another moment passed while neither of us spoke. I tipped my head back and looked up at the ceiling, while Peter rubbed out the tension at the back of his neck.

"You know," he said, "I always knew you guys shared something that I didn't really understand."

I looked up. "What do you mean?"

He shrugged. "When we were kids, there was something in the way you looked at each other. You never looked at me like that." He paused. "Sometimes I would see the two of you sitting together on the beach, and I didn't dare interrupt. I knew I couldn't possibly intrude on whatever it was you were talking about. Sometimes I was jealous and angry. Other times I was..."

He paused again, and I turned to face him. "You were what?"

"I was...*fascinated*. I wanted to know what it was like to be with you like that. I wanted to be close to you, like he was, but I didn't know how. I was glad when he left, because I knew that as long as he was around, you'd be with him and not me."

I swallowed over the lump of despair that was rising in my throat. "I'm sorry, Peter. I cared about you very much, and I still do. I never wanted to hurt you."

He dropped his gaze. "I know. Part of it's my own fault. I always knew that if I tried to take you away from him, I'd lose in the end. I knew you loved him. It was plain as day. I'm really sorry that this is happening."

I took a moment to digest all that he had confessed. "Thank you, Peter."

A janitor came around the corner, pushing a broom back and forth across the wide corridor. I watched him for a moment, then returned my attention to Peter.

"Can I ask you something?"

"Sure," he replied.

"What did you and Matt talk about when you were alone with him earlier?"

Peter drew in a breath. "Well...First he apologized for how he treated us in high school, when he ditched us for that other crowd."

"He said the same thing to me when he first came to Wellesley."

And I had known that he would need to say it to Peter.

"Then he told me that he was sorry for being the reason why you broke up with me, and that neither of you took any pleasure in hurting me – you especially. Then he told me that..." Peter hesitated. "That he was going to marry you."

I pushed away from the wall and regarded him with surprise. "He told you that?"

"Yeah, and I wanted to punch his lights out. If he wasn't hooked up to an IV, I probably would have."

I managed a small smile when Peter inclined his head and shrugged apologetically.

He cleared his throat and continued. "I figured that's what he wanted to say to me, when he sent you out of the room. I told him I wasn't surprised because I always knew you loved him more than you ever loved me."

"Peter..." I touched his shoulder, but he raised a hand to let me know he didn't welcome my pity.

"I told Matt that he better treat you right, and that if he ever hurt you, I'd make sure he regretted it. He accepted that."

"Peter..." I said again.

"No, Cora. Don't. Really. I want you to be happy. That's all."

I pulled him into my arms and hugged him. "I want you to be happy, too. I know you will be. I just don't think I'm the one for you."

"That's not true," he whispered in my ear. "I may not be the one for you, but you were always the one for me, and always will be."

I shut my eyes over the tears that stung my eyes, and kissed him on the cheek.

"So that's all you talked about?" I asked, as we started walking back to the chairs in the waiting area.

"No," he replied. "There was one more thing."

I stopped and took hold of his arm. "Tell me."

He looked down at the floor again. "Matt said that if anything happened to him, and he didn't make it through the surgery, that he wanted me to make sure you would be okay. So here I am." His eyes met mine. "I'm here for you, Cora, no matter what. But I want you to know that I really hope he makes it."

CHAPTER

Forty-eight

When the doors to the OR finally swung open, my whole being tightened with fear.

I stood up quickly and watched the surgeon walk the long length of the hall toward us. He kept his gaze downcast, and I knew in that moment that he did not have good news for us.

All the blood in my body rushed to my head. I couldn't seem to breathe.

"I'm very sorry," he said. "We did everything we could…"

Gordon bowed his head and wept, while Peter took me into his arms and whispered, "I'm so sorry, Cora. I'm so sorry."

Life

CHAPTER

Forty-nine

⁕

Sophie

I sat across the table from my mother and understood completely what she was feeling. I had experienced it myself, one year ago, in a New York hospital. The world had come to an end for me that day. The pain was more than anyone should ever have to endure.

"I'm sorry, Mom. I didn't know about any of that. Why didn't you ever tell me?"

"Because I was your mother, and I couldn't talk that way about a man who wasn't your father."

A surprising sense of calm descended upon me as I regarded her in the early evening light. "Because Matt was my real father, wasn't he?"

Mom pulled a tissue from the box and blew her nose. "Yes."

We sat for a long time saying nothing, while I waited for my mother to work through the grief she had just relived.

I stood up, went to the cupboard, and searched around until I found a bottle of brandy. I poured us each a small amount and sat back down.

"So obviously you married Dad after…" I paused. "After my real father died."

She raised the crystal tumbler to her lips, swirled the amber liquid around, and took a slow sip.

"After the operation," she said, "Peter was there for me in every way. He didn't pressure me to get back together with him. He was just there to comfort me, always a friend. He knew how I felt about Matt. He may not have truly understood it, but he knew how real it was.

"It wasn't easy, but I went back to Wellesley after Christmas and intended to finish out the year and get my degree. But after I started classes in January, I was sick in the mornings, and knew right away that I was pregnant."

She took another sip of brandy and looked at me solemnly from across the table. "It was the 60s," she explained. "It wasn't like it is today, and I was a Wellesley girl. I didn't know what my teachers or parents were going to say. I was a mess, Sophie, and I missed Matt so much, there were times I just wanted to curl up and die."

She paused. "At the same time, I was overjoyed that I was carrying his child. *You.* You were all I had left of him, and I was going to do whatever it took to keep you."

I frowned. "Whatever it took…Did you even tell Dad? Did he know what he was getting into? That you were already pregnant with Matt's baby? With *me?*"

I had a hard time comprehending it.

"Of course he knew," she said. "He was the one who suggested we get married. I didn't want to at first. I just couldn't bear the thought of marrying anyone except Matt. In my heart, he was already my husband, and I was his wife. I still loved him, but I also knew that I wouldn't be able to take care of you on my own. My parents would have pressured me to keep the whole thing a secret and give you up for adoption, then finish my degree. Peter knew how I felt about that. He knew I would never give you up. He worked hard to talk me into it, practically begged me to marry him, promised that he would love you like his own child.

"And he did, Sophie. He was a good husband and father. He loved you because you were a part of me – and God knows he loved me more than I ever deserved to be loved. He was my best friend, and I don't know how I would have survived without him."

She tipped the glass up and finished the brandy.

"Then why did you leave him?" I asked, feeling a sudden jolt of anger in my chest. "He didn't want you to leave. I heard you arguing about it in the days leading up to it, but you got on that plane, and you never came back. You left us. You left me. How could you do that? After everything you just told me, how could you abandon me? And Dad? He gave you everything."

She sat back in her chair and nodded. "Yes, he did, and I'm glad you understand that now, that you know what kind of man your father was, and still is. You were never close, I always knew that, but you didn't know the whole story. If your father was distant toward you, it was only because you reminded him of what he could never be to me. He always knew I loved Matt most, and then you. When Jen came along, that was different. She was our child together, and by that time, we had begun to build a real marriage." She leaned forward. "That's part of what you need to understand here today. Time does heal wounds. Eventually. The scars might remain, but life goes on. I loved Jen, and I loved your father. I always will. He was my hero. He never let me down. He never disappointed me, not once, and I will always be grateful to him for that."

I narrowed my eyes. "That still doesn't answer my question. If anything, I'm even more confused. Why did you leave us?"

She stood up. "I think you already know the answer to that question, Sophie. You've always known it, but you were confused when you came here. You don't understand where you are or what is happening to you."

My vision blurred. She wasn't clear to me. Nothing was.

I heard a creak on the stairs and felt a terrible compulsion to weep. "Is there someone else here?"

My mother nodded. "Yes."

I turned slowly in my chair and found myself staring at my daughter, Megan, who stood motionless in the doorway. Her brow furrowed with concern, and she spoke with a hint of anger. "I'm fine here, Mommy. I told you that. Nanny's taking good care of me. But you need to go back now. *Go back. Go back.*" She started to walk toward me, as if to push me away. She was annoyed with me.

I whirled around to face my mother. "Am I dead?"

"Not yet," she replied. "There's still time, but you must *want* to live."

Suddenly I was shooting through a dark, narrow tunnel, rounding a smooth curve. Graffiti lined the walls – which made no sense to me – and I was terrified by the speed at which I was traveling, and the strangeness of the place.

Was it a subway tunnel?

Where was I?

My eyes fluttered open and I blinked up at the bright blue sky. There were no clouds. It was a perfect day.

Was this heaven? How long had I been traveling? Was I really dead now?

I put my hand on my chest and massaged where it hurt. I walked my fingers across my ribcage, trying to identify the pain, then I struggled to sit up.

Looking all around, I realized I was sitting in a cemetery. The stone next to me said:

Cora MacIntosh

Beloved Wife and Mother

Sept 12, 1948 – Nov 17, 1984

Visions of my mother's funeral flashed like sparks of light through my brain, along with disturbing images of the plane crash, which we had seen on television.

My mother was dead. She didn't leave us by choice. I was wrong to blame her. She never meant to die.

I rose up onto my knees and ran my fingers over the letters and numbers chiseled into the stone. *Sept 12, 1948 – Nov 17, 1984*

Why did I never think of her, or talk about her? Why did I push this away?

"I'm sorry, Mom," I said, as I touched her name. Then I felt a hand on my shoulder and realized I was not alone.

Bewildered and slightly dizzy, I turned to look up. I lifted a hand to shade my eyes from the brightness of the sun.

"Hi Sophie," the man said. He was very handsome. "I think you might be lost. Please, let me help you."

He hooked an arm under mine and helped me to my feet.

S tanding at my mother's grave, I gazed into a pair of eyes the color of the ocean on a clear day. There was something familiar in them. I was spellbound.

"Who are you?" I asked, but somehow I already knew. This man was my father.

He smiled, and I understood immediately why my mother had fallen in love with him, and why they were meant to be together. I understood it in a way I never understood anything before, except for the love I felt for Megan on the day she was born. It happened instantaneously.

"You're Matt," I said, offering my hand.

He shook it. "And you're Sophie."

I laughed through joyful tears, wondering how any of this could be possible. I felt truly blessed.

"It's nice to meet you," he said. "I've been waiting a long time."

"Me too, I guess." I wasn't quite sure what to say.

He was very calm and serene. *Devastatingly beautiful.*

"Am I dead?" I asked.

"No. You're in the hospital right now. That's why your chest hurts. They're defibrillating you."

I massaged my heart again with the heel of my hand and glanced all around. "So I'm not really *here.*"

"Yes, you are."

More than a little confused, I squinted at him. "Where is *here* exactly? Am I in heaven?"

He shook his head. "No. Heaven's that way." He pointed toward the sky. "Closer to the blue."

I looked up. "I see."

And I did see. It was all so exquisite and breathtaking, the way the clouds rolled majestically before my eyes.

As a soft wave of understanding slowly rose within me, washing away all the panic and despair, I regarded my father affectionately in the bright sunshine.

"Walk with me," he said, and I followed.

Suddenly, we were strolling on a sandy beach, marveling at the thunder of the surf and the cries of the seabirds overhead. A strong, salty breeze cooled my cheeks.

"Megan told me to go back," I said, pushing a windblown lock of hair behind my ear. "But I'm not sure I want to. Being with her is all that matters to me. I think I'd rather stay here with her, and get to know *you*."

"Trust me," he said with a charismatic smile, "there will be plenty of time for that. It's my duty as your father to tell you that you still have work to do. You're not done yet."

"No?" I looked out at the water, then hopped over a foamy wave that slid up the beach and nearly soaked my feet.

My father stopped walking and met my gaze. "There are still some things you need to work out, Sophie. There are people you need to love for a little while longer."

"My dad," I said, feeling a rush of emotion in my heart. "*Peter.*"

He nodded, and we started walking again.

"There are others, too," he told me. "Don't give up hope. You never know what brilliant accomplishments might be in your future."

I nudged him with my elbow. "Do *you* know what those accomplishments are?"

He chuckled. "I know certain possibilities, because I've been watching your life, but only you can make them happen. You just need to recognize inspiration when it strikes. And be brave. Don't lose faith in the good things, even when life is tough. The good things come in waves, along with the bad."

I looked out at the water again as I considered his advice. "Well, after all of this – losing my daughter, my husband, crashing my car and dying – I can't imagine what else could be worse. Surely things can only get better from here."

"There, you see?" he said with a smile. "If you got through all this, you can get through anything. You're stronger than you think."

I linked my arm through his. "I'm starting to believe you. The story Mom told me, about you and her…It was beautiful. It made me remember what it feels like to be in love, and to feel inspired."

In a quiet flash, we were standing outside the hospital doors.

"Why didn't I know what was happening to me?" I asked. "Why didn't I know that Mom was dead, and that this wasn't real?"

"What do *you* think?"

I pondered it. "I was so angry with her for all those years. I needed to blame her for leaving us, because it was easier to be angry with her than it was to miss her. But all I ever wanted was to see her again and ask the questions she left unanswered – questions that were burning inside me. And I wanted to be with Megan."

"So you came here," he said, "but you didn't know where here was. It was too much for you to fully comprehend, that's all. It's not your fault. Death is…*strange.*"

I took a deep breath. "I didn't want to go back to my body, I know that much. Not after seeing Megan in the lake, which proved to me that there was something more beyond what we know. And I wanted so badly to see my mom again."

"Grief is difficult. You were only fourteen when she died, and your father took it hard. He packed all of you up and moved you to Augusta. Remember?"

I nodded.

"That's because your dad loved your mom very much, and it was hard for him. You should talk to him about it." Matt looked through the reflections in the glass doors. "Be good to him, okay? He's had it rough, too. You know how it feels to lose someone you love."

I fought back tears and nodded. "Thank you."

Rising up on my toes, I kissed him on the cheek. The sliding glass doors opened, and I stepped inside.

I turned back to look at him one last time, and he waved at me. His eyes were exactly the way Mom described them – as blue as the sea.

"See you around," I said, lifting a hand to wave good-bye.

His baby blues glimmered. "Definitely."

A light appeared behind him – a brilliant, dazzling light, more calming and loving than any words can possibly describe – and everything made sense to me as I watched him back into it.

I was no longer afraid, and I knew that everything would work out.

A heavy mist poured in through the open doors and the next thing I knew, I was lying flat on my back, listening to the steady beep of a heart monitor, while I blinked up at a clean white ceiling.

My lips cracked with dryness as I opened my mouth to speak. I felt as if I'd been hit by a truck, and couldn't form words.

Turning my head slightly on the pillow, I glanced up at two IV bags – one was clear and one was yellow – each dripping fluid into a tube that fed into my arm.

Suddenly, Dad's face appeared in front of me. Not the ghost of my biological father. This was Peter, the man who had raised me and loved me as his own.

Though I could not yet move, I felt a tremendous surge of joy skitter through my veins. I was alive, and my father was here, sitting at my bedside.

He touched his forehead to my shoulder and broke down in a fit of weeping.

I realized I had never seen him cry before, not even when Mom died. He had always worked so hard to be strong for us.

Patiently, I waited for him to compose himself. He lifted his head, wiped a sleeve across his whole face, then bolted for the door. "Nurse! Someone! My daughter's awake!"

Two nurses came running into the room. One of them checked the heart and oxygen monitors, while the other leaned over me. "Hello Sophie," she said. "Welcome back. Can you hear me?"

I managed to nod my head.

"That's good. Can you blink your eyes for me?"

I did that, too.

"Excellent. Now squeeze my hand. Very good. What about your toes? Can you wiggle them for me?"

I was able to do all the things she asked.

But she had one more question. "Do you know who I am?"

I shook my head. *No.* I'd never seen her before.

"I'm your nurse, Alice. Do you know who this man is?" She pointed at Dad, who was standing at the foot of the bed.

I worked very hard to move my lips and tongue, to take in enough air in order to push the words out – words I wanted very much to say out loud. When I finally spoke, I regarded him steadily. *"He's my father."*

There was a collective sigh of relief from everyone in the room. "She seems good," Alice said cheerfully, patting Dad on the shoulder. "This is wonderful."

He let out a tiny sob, mixed with laughter. "Yes."

"She'll be groggy for a little while, but that's normal. I'll send for the doctor and be back in a few minutes."

"Thank you."

He sat down next to me and took hold of my hand.

"How did you get here so fast?" My voice was weak. "Did you drive all the way from Augusta?"

"Yes, I came right away, as soon as Jen called and told me what happened. But you've been in a coma for a week, Sophie."

I blinked in surprise. "A week?"

"Yes. Do you remember anything? Do you know what happened to you?"

I stared uncertainly into his worried eyes. "I had a car accident."

But there was so much more…

"The driver behind you said you swerved to avoid hitting a deer. Do you remember that?"

I nodded. "My car rolled down the bank and landed on a frozen lake."

"That's right. The driver behind you called for help."

I began to wonder if it was all a dream. A week-long coma would provide more than enough time for the heavenly invention of elaborate scenarios about my dead mother and her tragic love life before I was born.

"Did I die?" I bluntly asked.

Dad hesitated, then answered my question. "Yes, Sophie, and it's a miracle that they were able to bring you back. A *miracle*."

My heart began to race. I thought back to the accident and everything I had witnessed from a place outside my body, and needed to know what really happened.

"I drowned, didn't I?"

"Yes, but you were hypothermic, thank God. That's the only reason they were able to save you. They brought you here in an ambulance and were able to resuscitate you after about forty minutes. Can you believe that, Sophie? Forty minutes. And here you are."

I struggled to get my bearings, for this was all so strange and inconceivable. "I guess a lot can happen in forty minutes." I wasn't sure if I should tell him what I'd experienced during that time – or what I *think* I experienced. I still wasn't completely certain.

"Could I have a drink of water?" I asked. My mouth was still dry, and my head was throbbing.

He went to the bathroom and ran the tap, then returned with a paper cup and a straw which he held to my lips. I lifted my head to take a small drink, and relaxed back down on the pillow.

"Thank you." Feeling tired all of a sudden, I closed my eyes.

Megan's image – standing in the doorway of my mother's house –appeared in my mind. *I'm okay here,* she had said to me. *Nanny's taking good care of me.*

An unexpected sense of calm moved through me, and I began to believe that I really had traveled to heaven – or someplace between here and there.

Opening my eyes, I glanced up at my father. "I'm glad you're here. It means a lot to me."

"Of course I'm here," he replied, almost laughing as he sat back down. "I know I haven't been the best father to you, Sophie, but I couldn't bear it if I lost you. You and Jen...You're all I have.

I squeezed his hand. "But you *were* the best father," I told him. "And it was my fault, too, because I wasn't the best daughter. I was rebellious and headstrong and I just think...after Mom died...you and I became disconnected."

He bowed his head and nodded.

"Why didn't we ever talk about her?" I asked.

He looked away and mulled over the question for a moment. "It hurt too much, I guess, so I thought it would be better not to." He met my gaze. "And I blamed myself for what happened to her. I thought everything was my fault, and I didn't want to admit that to you and Jen. I was afraid you'd hate me."

"How could it have been your fault? It was a plane crash."

He sighed heavily. "We argued about her leaving. She wanted to drive to Chicago, but that meant she'd be gone for a week. I didn't want her to go – I never did – so she compromised that time by saying she'd fly and be back in twenty-four hours."

I swallowed uneasily. No wonder he had withdrawn from us after the accident. He had been harboring this guilt for a very long time.

"Tell me more about that," I said, encouraging him to continue. "I never understood why she wanted to go to Chicago by herself all those times. For years afterward, I thought she must have been having an affair. I heard you arguing about it. I knew those trips of hers pulled you apart." I paused. "But she wasn't having an affair, was she?"

"No."

He wouldn't look at me, so I laid my hand on his cheek and spoke softly. "It's okay, Dad. You can tell me the truth now. I'm a grown-up. I can take it."

Still, he wouldn't answer me. He kept his eyes lowered, so I revealed the truth for him.

"I'm not your real daughter, am I?"

He swallowed hard and shook his head.

I felt a tremendous sense of relief.

"I always knew Mom was pregnant when you married her," I said, "but she was pregnant by someone *else*, wasn't she?"

At last, his watery eyes lifted, and he gazed at me with apology and remorse. "I know how it must seem to you, Sophie, but it wasn't like that. Your mother loved that man very much and she would have married him, but he died, sweetheart. That's why she went to Chicago every year in November. To visit his grave. I'm sorry. I should have told you a long time ago."

"It's okay, Dad." I squeezed his hand. "I'm just glad to know it now. And what you did for Mom – the way you loved her all those years, and took care of us...You were her hero, and you're mine, too. You'll always be my hero."

He stood to gather me into his arms, and told me that he loved me.

Whatever disconnection existed between us in the past began to fall away. I felt, deep in my heart, that I understood him now. I felt very close to him.

"Does Jen know that we're half-sisters?" I carefully asked, as Dad sat down again.

"No. I never told anyone."

"Well, I think we should tell her. I know she'll understand when she hears the whole story."

He continued to hold my hand, then suddenly he frowned.

"What's wrong?" I asked. "You don't want me to tell her?"

"It's not that. I'm just confused. I don't understand something." He scrutinized my face.

"What?"

"How did you know you died? Because you never regained consciousness. Or did you?

I wet my lips and contemplated how best to answer the question.

"I'm not really sure you'd believe it if I told you. I still don't quite believe it myself."

"Try me."

For a few seconds, I stared at him and considered peddling backwards over my words. I could tell him that I did wake briefly, and one of the nurses told me what happened.

But what if he asked how I knew about Mom and Matt? Part of me wanted desperately to tell him the truth. I wanted to ask him more questions about that time in his life, and I wanted to tell someone about my experiences at the bottom of the lake, when I watched my body convulse and go still, just before I took part in a conversation with my daughter, who had been dead for a year.

And what about the ride in the ambulance? I had every intention of seeking out the paramedic whose dog had died and was brought back to life. I wanted to ask her questions and cross-check my own memories and observations with what she remembered about the drive to the hospital.

I wanted answers. Proof.

Then I realized there was a much easier way to determine whether or not I had actually visited my dead mother in some alternate, heavenly dimension.

"Dad," I said. "Tell me something."

"Okay."

I managed to lean up on one elbow. "The first time you kissed Mom…Where were you?"

His expression softened, and he looked toward the window as he remembered it. "We were at the lake near our old house in Camden. It was the first warm day of spring, and we had just gone for a swim. I was fifteen years old."

A shiver of happiness rippled up my spine, and goose bumps covered my body. "Yes, that's right," I said with a smile, nodding my head at him.

He looked at me strangely and I knew in that moment that I was going to tell him everything.

Because we were no longer disconnected.

D ad had no choice but to believe me after I was able to describe the most intimate details about his courtship with Mom, including their break-up and what happened in the hospital when Matt went in for surgery. There was no way I could have known these things unless Mom had told me, and he knew she hadn't, at least not when she was alive.

(Later, when I was fully recovered, I was interviewed by an endless parade of doctors and experts on the subject of near-death experiences, including a scholar from Germany who was writing a book and wanted to include my story in his research. I also made appearances on a few network talk shows. But I'm getting ahead of myself.)

When I finished telling Dad about my experiences "on the other side," he called Jen right away and asked her to come to the hospital.

She arrived a short while later and burst into tears when she saw me sitting up, eating lunch.

Dad left us alone and went home to her place to take a shower.

I decided to wait before I told her the whole story and divulged the fact that we were only half-sisters because our mother had once loved another man. I just wanted to visit with her for a while.

Turns out I'm glad I waited, because Jen had something equally important to tell me, and she could barely contain herself.

"There's something you should know," she said as she rolled the lunch table away from my bed.

"Sounds like juicy gossip."

She bit her lip and nodded.

"Well, spit it out then."

She continued to keep me waiting, as if she wasn't sure how to explain whatever it was she needed to tell me.

"Hey," I said. "I died last week, remember? Whatever it is, it can't possibly be any more shocking than that. Seriously, at this point, I can take anything you throw at me, so give it your best."

She chuckled. "It's not a *bad* thing. In fact, I think it's really sweet, but you might be creeped out, that's all."

"Jen, I promise you, after what I've been through, nothing is going to creep me out."

She sat down in the chair by the bed and her cheeks flushed with color. "You know how Dad told you that he and I took turns sitting by your side since the night of the accident?"

I nodded.

"Well, it wasn't just the two of us. You had another visitor, too. Someone who was very devoted, and came every night after supper."

My attention floated to all the flower arrangements on the windowsill, and those on the far table. I hadn't looked at any of the cards yet.

"Was it Michael?" But I found that difficult to imagine. He hated hospitals, and his cheery, bouncy fiancée was due to give birth fairly soon.

"No, it wasn't Michael. It was Kirk Duncan."

She might as well have tossed a glass of water in my face. I was, indeed, that shocked.

I sat straight up. "Really?"

I hadn't seen Kirk since the year after he left for college. We'd exchanged emails a few times, of course, but that was it.

"Kirk was here? In this room?"

"Yes. Every night for a week. I suspect he'll be here again tonight, unless I call him and tell him you're awake. Then he might come sooner. Or not at all. Who knows?"

I was flattered and touched, and slightly giddy at the notion that my high school sweetheart had come to my so-called deathbed.

"Wow," I said. "I guess I was wrong about not being surprised. I'm speechless."

"I can see that," Jen replied. "I knew you would be."

Tipping my head back on the pillow, I wondered what he looked like now. Did he still have all his hair? Had his smile changed?

"I'm going to need to brush my teeth," I said, in a bit of a dazed stupor. "And take a shower." I looked around for the call button. "Can we get a nurse in here? I'll need some help."

Jen stood up. "I've got it covered. Nurse!" she shouted. "We need some help in here!"

An older, heavy-set nurse came running into the room. "What is it?" Her eyes darted to the heart monitor, then back at me.

"Don't worry," Jen said. "She's still alive, but she needs to get cleaned up and get her hair washed. Maybe put on some makeup."

The nurse folded her arms. "This isn't a beauty spa, ladies. It's a hospital, and we're short-staffed today. We'll get around to you eventually."

Jen boldly approached her. "I don't think you understand." She pointed at me. "That woman's high school sweetheart could be here at any moment, and she hasn't seen him in years. And she was *dead* a week ago!"

The nurse peered around Jen's shoulder to take a look at me. "Does she mean the guy who was here last week? The one with the guitar?"

I felt a tingling heat spread to my cheeks. "He brought his guitar?"

Jen spoke over her shoulder. "Yes, and he played for you."

"That's just so Kirk."

The nurse moved around Jen and stood at the foot of my bed. "How many years has it been since you've seen this man?"

"About twenty."

Her shoulders rose and fell with a deep sigh of defeat, then she marched around the bed and folded back the covers. "Well, get up then, princess. We can't have you smelling like a coma patient when Romeo arrives." She glanced at Jen. "Do you have some lipstick? Maybe a little blush? She's still a bit pale."

"Oh yes," Jen replied, pulling an enormous cosmetic bag out of her purse. "I have *everything*."

Fifty-three

J en called Kirk that afternoon to tell him the good news – that I was out of the coma and doing just fine.

He was pleased to hear it and promised to come by after work.

Sure enough, shortly after I finished my supper on a tray, a knock rapped lightly at the door.

Jen gave me a look, then called out, "Come in!"

Suddenly there he was – Kirk, my first love, wearing a soft brown leather jacket and jeans, his guitar case slung across his back.

My heart skipped a beat at the sight of him. He still looked exactly the same. He hadn't aged a day, except for a few strands of grey in his wavy brown hair.

My whole body warmed with affection, and his eyes lit up with joy.

"Oh, wow." He shook his head in disbelief and gestured toward me with a hand. "I don't think I've ever been so happy to see somebody awake."

I smiled. "Hi Kirk."

He set his guitar case on the floor and approached the bed. He sat down on the edge of it. "Thank God you're okay."

"I'm fine now." I held out my arms. "But I could use a hug." He leaned closer, and we embraced.

"It's so good to see you," I whispered. "I can't believe you're here."

"I prayed every day."

I was vaguely aware of Jen discreetly tiptoeing out of the room.

Sitting back, Kirk continued to hold my hand. "You look terrific."

"So do you. Jen told me you were here this week, and that you played your guitar for me. I wish I could remember. I hate the fact that I missed it."

"Don't worry about it. I can play for you anytime, and I suspect you'll be a much better audience now."

We were both quiet for a moment.

"It's been a rough year for you, hasn't it?" he said.

I glanced down at our joined hands. "Yes, it has."

"Well…the way I see it, things can only get better from here."

I thought of what Matt had said to me on the other side, and smiled. "I'm sure you're right about that."

Suddenly I felt a wave of emotion rise up inside me, and my heart beat fast with anticipation. I was so grateful to be alive. To have been given a second chance at finding happiness again.

"At least I'm still here," I said. "Though I'm not sure what I did to deserve such a miracle."

"It must have been one heck of a miracle," he replied. "Forty minutes, Sophie. You came back after forty minutes. That's got to be a record."

I laughed. "Crazy, isn't it?"

"It's insane. But you always were a fighter."

"I guess so."

"So what was it like?" he asked. "Do you remember anything? Did you see a white light? Or maybe you'd prefer not to talk about it."

Looking into his familiar green eyes, I realized that the passing of time meant very little in relation to the soul. I had not seen this man for almost twenty years, but it felt as if we had been together the entire time, and had not spent a single day apart. I was as comfortable with him now as I had been when we were a couple, intimately in love. I trusted him wholeheartedly and knew that he would never let me down.

"I *would* like to talk about it with you," I said. "But maybe another time, if that's okay. After I get out of here. Right now, I just want to hear about *you*." Feeling tired all of a sudden, I rested my head on the pillow. "Tell me about your life. Are you still teaching music? I want to know everything. Don't leave anything out."

He stared into my eyes for the longest time, then leaned close and kissed me on the cheek. "I've really missed you, Sophie. I'm glad you came back."

I wrapped my arms around his neck and whispered into his ear. "Me, too."

That one special moment, all on its own, was worth coming back for.

Then I remembered what Matt had said to me on the beach, and I was confident that there would be more moments like this in my future. The good and the bad – it would all come in waves.

CHAPTER

Fifty-four

❦

I spent another week in the hospital, recovering from the accident and slowly regaining my strength.

Kirk visited me each night, and almost immediately, there was an unspoken understanding between us – that we were entering into another long-term, committed relationship that would probably last forever this time.

As I said before, it felt like not a single day had passed since high school, when we were head over heels in love with each other, and shared the same values and desires. This time we were going to leap in with both feet. I had no doubts or fears. It simply felt right on every level, and when I was finally able to go home, he was the one who picked me up and drove me to Jen's house.

Very quickly, however, we decided that life was too short, so I moved in with him a week later.

My story doesn't end here, however. There's still so much more to tell.

CHAPTER

Fifty-five

I mentioned that people were curious about my death and out-of-body experience, and for a while I was willing to participate in interviews and medical studies. But it soon grew exhausting, and I just wanted to live my life. I was a writer, and if you've ever known a writer intimately – or if you *are* one – you will understand that we are a different breed. Writing is a solitary occupation, and we like it that way.

All I wanted to do after I recovered was tell my story, but not in front of cameras or live audiences. I needed peace and quiet if I was going to find the right words.

So here we are. As you can see, by the evidence before you, I returned to writing and remembered how to put words, even difficult ones, down on paper.

But again, I'm getting ahead of myself.

Before I wrote this story, I worked on something else – something very different, which garnered great critical acclaim.

That story will always hold a special place in my heart, for it was the compass that pointed me back to the true essence of my life.

Spring came early that year. When the snow and ice melted and a scented breeze blew across the front veranda of Kirk's country house one warm Sunday afternoon, we decided to take a trip to the Cape and book ourselves into a quaint little B&B, drink lots of wine, and stroll along the beach for three glorious days.

It was just what I needed to mark the end of my recovery. Time alone with Kirk, my first love, who had never left my heart.

Time to appreciate the splendor of the life I had not squandered, and to comprehend the magic of the sea, the earth, and sky.

Each night, while the surf thundered wondrously outside our window, we made love with great tenderness and passion.

This was it – *real love* – a lifetime of it, exploding out of my soul. At last we were together, home in each other's arms after too many years apart.

But this time we were grown-ups, and nothing was going to tear us apart.

On our last night at the inn, Kirk took my hand and led me onto the beach for a last midnight stroll. The moon was full and bright, reflecting off the dark water, and the waves spread across the sand with smooth, glistening freedom.

"Sophie," Kirk whispered in my ear.

Just the sound of my name on his lips sent a feverish swell of desire down the length of my body.

He slid his hand around my waist and pulled me close. "You know I love you. I always have, and always will. So please..." He got down on one knee, took both my hands in his, and kissed my open palms. "Marry me, Sophie. Be my wife. Stay with me forever, because I don't ever want to be without you again."

All the joy in the universe descended upon me in that incredible moment, and I laughed joyfully through my tears. "Of course I'll marry you." I dropped to my knees as well on the cool, shifting sand. "You're the great love of my life. I know it now, more surely than anything."

We were married two weeks later in a small civil ceremony on the back lawn of our country home, and as soon as school let out, we traveled to the Greek island of Santorini for our honeymoon.

CHAPTER

Fifty–seven

⤛⟡⤜

In September of that year, I woke one morning with a dream in my head. Or rather, the vivid recollection of a moment in my mother's kitchen, when she shared a specific detail with me:

Over the next five days, Matt and I spent every possible moment together. He wouldn't let me skip any classes, so he dropped me off five minutes before class began, and was there outside the building waiting for me when I came out.

If I had assignments or papers to write, he took me to the library, sat next to me, and worked on finishing his own book while I studied or researched.

I remembered my father's words on the beach. *You just need to recognize inspiration when it strikes.*

I had been waiting a long time for such a lightning strike, for the motivation to return to my writing, and suddenly there it was – not so much like a bolt of lightning, but like a star falling out of the sky and landing on my lap.

Tossing the covers aside, I leaped out of bed. A few seconds later, I was dialing my father's number in Augusta.

"Dad, when we moved out of the house in Camden, what happened to all the stuff in the attic? The boxes and trunks full of papers? It was mostly Mom's stuff – her college assignments and memorabilia. Did we get rid of it?"

"Of course not," he replied. "I saved everything. I couldn't very well part with it, now could I?"

My heart began to beat wildly. "So it's there at your place?"

"Yes. I'm looking up at the ceiling right now. It's all there, over my head."

I smiled. "Can I come and see you, and go through some of it?"

He paused. "You sound excited. Are you looking for something special?"

"Yes." I told him what it was, and he whistled into the phone. "I'll be there soon," I said.

"I'll be waiting for you."

There was no proper staircase to Dad's attic, only a square door in the upper hall ceiling with a ladder that folded down on rusty hinges.

I had not gone into the attic since I was fourteen years old. After we had carried all of Mom's things up that rickety ladder, we closed the door behind us and that was the end of it. We forced ourselves to forget it was ever there, to pretend it didn't exist.

But it did exist. It was right there above us all these years.

Carefully I climbed up and peered around the small space under my father's peaked roof. A tiny oval window provided some light. It smelled musty and old.

"Pass me the flashlight," I said to him. He didn't trust the ladder and was holding it steady with one hand while he bent down to pick up the light with the other. He handed it to me and I switched it on.

A long ray of white light dashed across the wooden beams on the slanted roof while I climbed the rest of the way up and rose to my feet.

I looked at all the boxes of books, the suitcases full of her clothes.

Suddenly, she was all around me. I could feel her presence, her affection and love. Somehow I knew she was pleased that I was here.

Dad popped his head up. "Wow. There's a lot of stuff up here. I'd forgotten…"

"You aren't kidding. You *did* save everything."

He continued to glance over the trunks and boxes. "I just couldn't bring myself to throw anything away."

I smiled down at him. "I'm glad."

For the next hour, we dug through Mom's belongings. I found much of my own things mixed in – my elementary school projects and report cards, and four years of costumes from tap and ballet classes.

I came to a bankers' box full of old photo albums and journeyed back in time to the family camping trips I had all but forgotten about. The Christmas mornings. The Easter egg hunts in the backyard.

We'd had a good life together – Mom, Dad, Jen and me. It was a shame we had never talked about it, never celebrated it.

The last album I came to, at the bottom of the box, looked different from the others.

It was not from my childhood.

It was from my mother's.

Slowly I opened to the first page and glided my fingers over a black-and-white photograph of Mom as a baby on a bright summer day, taking a bath outside in a round steel tub. Behind her, there were sheets hanging on a clothesline, blowing in the wind. Beyond was the sea.

On the pages that followed, there were photos of Mom as a child with her family. At last I came upon a picture of her with my two fathers – Peter and Matt. They were, all three of them, sitting on their bikes, smiling into the camera.

I felt a rush of contentment in the knowledge that I knew the truth about my mother's life. That I understood where I came from.

Then I found something that made the tiny hairs on my neck stand on end.

It was a photograph of Mom and Matt together in a playground, side by side on two swings. They couldn't have been more than five or six years old. My grandmother stood behind Mom, pushing her.

Behind Matt, an attractive, dark-haired young woman was laughing and holding onto her hat. It was a wide-brimmed straw hat that I had seen before.

"Dad, who is this?" I handed him the album. "The woman in the hat."

He squinted through his bifocals. "That's Matt's mother." He glanced across at me. "She died when he was young. Just seven or eight. She fell down a flight of stairs."

I took hold of the album again and stared in awe at the picture. "That would make her my grandmother."

He removed his glasses. "Yes, it would."

Catherine.

"She was a gardener, wasn't she?" A warm glow sparked within me.

"That's right. When she was alive, they had the best yard on the street. How do you know this?"

I slowly turned the page. "It's part of what happened to me. I didn't mention it before. There were too many other things to tell you about. But she was there when I visited Mom. She was her neighbor and she was planting a garden. She wore that same hat."

Dad simply nodded, and we went back to our searching.

At last I found what I was looking for. My father's manuscript, buried in a mountain of term papers and projects that my mother had completed at Wellesley.

It was held together by a string – hundreds of sheets of lined loose leaf, filled with words handwritten in pencil by my father.

"I found it."

Plunking myself down on top of a trunk, I removed the string and flipped to the first page.

"Wait a second...Please stop." Dad rose to his feet. I looked up at him with curious eyes, wondering if he meant to warn me about something.

"You shouldn't start reading that here," he said. "You'll ruin your eyes. Bring it downstairs. You can use my desk, and I'll make you a pot of coffee."

For a few startled seconds I blinked up at him, then I smiled. "You're right, Dad. I'll need more light."

I gathered the treasure in my arms, and followed him to the ladder.

CHAPTER

Fifty-eight

❧

I stayed up all night reading my father's manuscript, which he had managed to complete a mere week before his death.

As I composed myself and wiped the last few tears from my cheeks, I sat back in the chair and wondered what I was going to do with it. There could be no denying that it was a literary masterpiece, but it was about two hundred pages too long and written by an author who wasn't alive to edit it or submit it to agents or publishers.

It seemed an overwhelming task, and what if I was wrong? What if it wasn't as good as I thought? Or what if I ruined it by making changes?

Those were just my own insecurities talking, however. Deep down, I knew exactly what I had to do to make it better, and in that moment – as I felt the rush of my father's blood coursing through my veins – I was absolutely certain that I could accomplish it.

Suddenly he was there in the room with me, telling me to go to bed and rest my eyes. Sleep on it.

I could hear his voice: *Think about the story, Sophie. It needs a lot of work. I wish I'd had time to fix it, but it just wasn't possible. Take it home with you and talk it over with your husband, then get to work. You'll know what to do.*

CHAPTER

Fifty-nine

⤬⤬⤬

Two months later, I sent the full, revised manuscript – now typed and double-spaced in Courier font – to five top New York agents, who all requested it based on my query letter and synopsis.

I felt confident. I had worked in the publishing industry in the past, so I knew the lay of the land. I had selected agents who represented similar projects and had sold them for respectable advances.

My father's book was brilliant. How could it not succeed?

My only concern was the fact that he was not alive to represent himself, and these days, publishers were looking for a promotable author, someone who could appear before the reading public through websites, social media, and talk-show interviews.

What I was attempting to do was a bit unusual. I was hoping to generate excitement over a debut author who had been dead for forty years.

Of course I would have been happy to represent him myself, and with my recent notoriety due to the accident and my infamous other-worldly experience, I thought I might be able to offer some unique opportunities for publicity. At this point, all I could do was cross my fingers.

And wait for a nibble from an agent.

_6

Three weeks after I sent out the proposals for my father's book, I received my first reply. The envelope arrived in our mailbox by snail mail, which was unexpected, since most correspondence with publishers occurred through email these days. I took it as a good omen.

Kirk handed the envelope to me when I exited the shower after a late-afternoon run.

The return address indicated that it had come from the agent at the top of my list – a real heavy-hitter when it came to book and movie deals.

I stood in the kitchen in my white terrycloth robe, my wet hair twisted over my head and wrapped in a blue towel.

"What if they hated it?" I asked, glancing across the table at Kirk, who was dipping an herbal teabag into a mug of steaming water he had just poured from the kettle.

"Then you'll try again, and next time, pick someone with better taste.

Kirk had read the manuscript and helped me decide how to edit a few things. He, too, recognized its brilliance.

Nevertheless, I had a knot in my stomach the size of the state of Idaho.

"*You* open it." I circled around the table and held out the letter.

He raised his hands as if I were pointing a gun. "Oh no, not me. I'm here to congratulate you, or be a shoulder to cry on. I don't want to be the messenger."

"Please?" I tried to make him take it – I practically shoved it into his hands – and bless his heart, he couldn't say no to me.

"Are you sure you don't want to be the first one to read it?"

I considered it for a moment, then slowly plucked it out of his hands. "I think maybe I do."

Turning away, I walked to the window and slid my finger under the flap, then carefully tore the paper.

My heart pounded as I unfolded the reply, which was printed on expensive agency letterhead.

Dear Ms. Duncan,

Thank you for your recent submission. Though there was much to admire in the story and writing, I'm afraid we cannot offer representation at this time. Good luck placing your work elsewhere.

Sincerely,
Jo Sanderson
Sanderson Literary Agency

I turned and faced my husband, and slowly shook my head. "He said no."

Before I knew it, Kirk was taking me into his arms and rubbing his hands up and down my back. "Are you okay?"

"Yeah, just disappointed, that's all."

"This is only the first one. This guy's not the only agent in New York. The book is good, Sophie. Someone will want it."

"I hope so."

"Well, I know so."

I pulled the towel off my head and used it to squeeze out the dampness in my hair.

"Can I do anything for you?" Kirk asked. "Make you a cup of tea?"

I looked into the deep green of his eyes and felt my disappointment taking a back seat to the love I felt for him.

"A glass of wine would be nice, if you'll have one with me."

He looked me up and down. "Are you naked under that robe?"

I nodded. "Naked, and still a little bit wet."

Kirk chuckled. "Then I think I'll definitely pop the cork on something."

A short while later, he joined me in our king-size bed and all thoughts of rejection vanished from my mind as he untied my robe and slid his hands across my stomach.

Three days later, I walked into the supermarket and stopped dead in my tracks when I smelled something strange and disgusting. Something I didn't recognize.

I couldn't quite describe it, but it was a nauseating combination of aromas: a teenager's stinky socks, and warm, rotting meat.

Fighting the urge to gag, I covered my nose and mouth with a hand, turned around and hurried out.

For a long while I stood on the sidewalk, watching the world go by, then marched two doors down to the pharmacy, where I hunted up and down the aisles.

Five minutes later, I walked out of there with a pregnancy test and a very powerful urge to pee.

CHAPTER

Sixty-one

༄ ᶜᶜᴖᴖᴖ

"**C**ongratulations," the doctor said, folding his hands on his desk. "You're going to have a baby."

Kirk covered my hand with his and gently squeezed it, while I waded through the confusing tidal wave of my emotions.

My first thought, of course, was for Megan. A part of me didn't want to have another child – a child who would fill up the empty space in my heart that still belonged only to her.

Another part of me was terrified. I was forty years old. What if something went wrong? What if this baby got sick, or had some sort of accident? I wasn't sure I could survive the loss of another child.

Those thoughts and feelings, however, were fleeting. Kirk's hand was warm upon mine, and the love I felt for him – and the love I felt from him in return – eclipsed all the old fears that had been lingering quietly on the outer fringes of my world.

A child…

A child with Kirk, who would be there for us both. Forever. In good times, and in bad.

I thought of my mother and all that she had suffered when she lost the man she loved – yet she'd gone on to live a happy life, to raise Jen and me, to love and respect the man who was at her side so devotedly. The old photo albums were proof of it, as was my rekindled relationship with my father, who I now cherished more than ever before.

It was indeed possible to start again, to find joy, even after it seemed lost forever.

Happy tears filled my eyes and spilled onto my cheeks as I turned toward Kirk. "A baby," I said, laughing. "We're going to have a baby."

His face split into a wide grin, which completely dazzled me. I felt as if I were floating.

The doctor smiled at us as we embraced, and I knew that everything was going to be okay. *More* than okay, because we had each other.

"Do you think it'll be a boy or a girl?" Kirk asked me that night as he lay beside me in bed.

"It's definitely going to be a boy," I replied.

"You're that sure? Do you have a crystal ball or something?"

"Sort of." I rolled to face him. "Remember when I told you about seeing Megan at the bottom of the lake, and that she spoke to me?"

"Yes. She told you there was something you needed to do."

"That's right, but she said something else. I didn't tell you because I was afraid I might jinx it, or maybe I just wasn't sure I understood her correctly."

"What did she say?"

I leaned up on an elbow. "She told me that I couldn't follow her to heaven yet because I needed to take care of her brother."

Kirk sat up as well and regarded me with fascination. "No kidding."

"I told her, of course, that she didn't *have* a brother, but she explained to me that he was waiting for his turn. So...I think we're going to have a son."

Kirk stared at me in disbelief. Then he inched closer on the bed and kissed me on the mouth.

If happiness comes in waves, my life was bobbing about in a
thrilling and terrifying windstorm at sea.

The day after the doctor confirmed that I was pregnant, the
telephone rang. Kirk was at work, and I was home alone.

According to the call display, it was a 212 area code, which
meant it was coming from New York.

Every nerve ending in my body tensed suddenly. What if it
was one of the agents who had read Matt's book? What if this
person was calling to offer representation? They didn't usually
call to reject you.

After the third ring, I braced myself for anything, and picked
up the phone. "Hello?"

"Is this Sophie Duncan?" It was a man's voice.

"Yes, may I help you?"

There was a brief pause, then a click, which told me I had just
been taken off speaker phone.

"Well, hello there," the caller said cheerfully. "This is Dennis
Velcoff from Phoenix Literary. You submitted your father's book to us."

I sat down. "Yes, that's right. It's nice to hear from you, Mr.
Velcoff. What can I do for you?"

He paused again. "I think the more important question is
what I can do for *you*, Ms. Duncan, because I really loved the

book. It's the best thing to come across my desk in a dog's age. I'd like to talk to you about representation. Do you have a minute?"

I began to quietly tap my feet on the floor, while I fought to keep my voice calm. "Of course."

He launched into a detailed speech about all the things he loved in the book – the tragic elements of the story, the strength of the characters, the lyrical quality of the prose. He felt that it was not only a literary masterpiece, but that it had commercial value as well, which was a rare combination, and he was certain the plot would do well in the hands of a good screenwriter.

Mr. Velcoff wanted my permission to send it over to a Hollywood film agent.

In the meantime, while Hollywood was looking at it, Mr. Velcoff wanted to shop it around to the right people in New York, and get me a book deal. He was absolutely certain he could get at least six figures for it – possible seven if the stars aligned just right.

Was I interested? he asked. I had to pick myself up off the floor in order to say yes.

Three weeks later, after a fierce bidding war between three large publishing houses, the deal closed at half-a-million dollars for the North American print rights, while Mr. Velcoff held onto the foreign rights. He intended to start selling those as soon as the offer for the film rights was nailed down.

An A-list producer did, indeed, want to adapt it to film, and at that point, he and Mr. Velcoff were still negotiating the deal.

The following day, I was offered a million dollars for the film option, and I happily took the check – which I donated, in equal amounts, to the oncology department at the children's hospital where Megan was treated, and neurological cancer research.

With great pleasure, I placed the donations in Megan's and my father's names.

CHAPTER

Sixty-three

If you're reading this book, you've probably already guessed that Mr. Velcoff represented me on this project as well, which also went for a significant advance. You can hunt around for the exact dollar amount on the Internet if you're curious.

But let me remind you that it really doesn't matter. I would have written this book for nothing, for it was a story I simply had to tell.

Epilogue

I am pleased to report that I gave birth to a healthy son and we named him Peter Matthew Duncan.

A year and a half later, Kirk and I had a second child – a daughter we named Cora.

These days, we live a happy, quiet life at our home in the New Hampshire countryside. Kirk still teaches music and occasionally plays a gig at a jazz club in the city.

I'm a full-time mother and part-time writer, who has learned to appreciate the small, special moments which never fail to take my breath away.

I still miss Megan. Sometimes I ache to hold her in my arms, watch her sleep, smell the sweet scent of her skin. I wish I could watch her grow into a beautiful young woman and seek out her destiny. She would be in middle school now if she had not departed from this world, but that is not how things are, and I know I must accept it.

So, I do. I look at her picture on my desk and feel the spirit of her presence. I savor the love she left behind.

That will have to be enough, at least until we meet again.

So we are done now, I believe. That was my story, but I have no intention of typing THE END, because I no longer believe in such a thing. Hope lives forever.

Thank you for sharing this journey with me.
I wish you happiness and joy.

Questions for Discussion

1. In chapter one, Sophie mentions her first love, Kirk Duncan, and says: "I knew that no matter where life took us, I would always love him." Do you believe she made a mistake to let him go? Was her marriage to Michael a mistake?

2. Sophie's husband Michael wants to have another child when Megan is ill. Do you think Sophie was right to say no, and do you think it would have made a difference in keeping their marriage together if she had gotten pregnant at that time?

3. When Sophie rekindles her romance with Kirk after she wakes up in the hospital, do you believe it was the right thing for her to do, or do you feel she was playing it safe, retreating into a former, familiar comfort zone?

4. Different sections of the book have different headings: Sunshine and Rain, Going Home, Cora's Story, Flowers, The Deep Blue Sea, Mountains, Life. What is the significance of these headings in terms of the story structure and the themes?

5. In chapter thirty-two, just before Matt walks back into Cora's life, she says: "It was early October in 1968 when the monstrous wave crashed and exploded onto the coastline of my life, changing my future forever." Earlier in chapter twenty-nine, not long after she and Peter share their first kiss at the

lake, she says: "The woods were quiet that day. I couldn't hear the sea." What is the significance of these two ideas in relation to Peter and Matt, and where else in the novel does "land and sea" play a part in terms of symbolism? What does this reveal about Cora and what she wants out of life?

6. Peter quickly comes to Cora's rescue after Matt's death, and offers her marriage. Do you think she was right to accept him? Did you feel that Peter was taken advantage of, or did you view him as a heroic character?

7. When Sophie leaves the hospital to return to her mother's house in Camden, did you know that she was still having an out-of-body experience? At what point in the novel did you realize that Cora was dead and the Camden world was not real? What were some early clues that suggested it was an out-of-body experience?

8. Grief is an important theme in the novel. How does it affect Sophie's relationship with her father, Peter, and how does it affect the breakdown of her marriage? What were some similarities in these two relationships? Do you believe Sophie and Kirk will be able to weather future storms in their marriage if grief becomes an issue?

9. How does the discovery of Matt's manuscript in Peter's attic change Sophie's life? Do you think Matt wanted her to publish his novel? Why or why not?

10. Do you believe in life after death? Have you ever had an out-of-body experience or some communication with a "ghost," or do you know someone who has?

11. In the epilogue, Sophie reveals that she had a son with Kirk – which is exactly what Megan predicted. Sophie then goes on to say they also had a daughter, but Megan never mentioned a sister. What do you think is the significance of this?

For more information about this book and others in the Color of Heaven series, please visit the author's website at www. juliannemaclean.com. While you're there be sure to sign up for Julianne's newsletter to be notified about when a new book in this series is released.

Read on for an excerpt from *The Color of Destiny*, book two in the Color of Heaven series.

The COLOR of DESTINY

Book Two
Available Now

Eighteen years ago a teenage pregnancy changed Kate Worthington's life forever. Faced with many difficult decisions, she chose to follow her heart and embrace an uncertain future with the father of her baby and her devoted first love.

At the same time, in another part of the world, sixteen-year-old Ryan Hamilton makes his own share of mistakes, but learns important lessons along the way. Twenty years later, Kate's and Ryan's paths cross in a way they never could have expected, which makes them question the possibility of destiny. Even when all seems hopeless, could it be that everything happens for a reason, and we end up exactly where we are meant to be?

~⸱

Preface

⟡

Kate Worthington

According to Webster's Dictionary, destiny is defined as a predetermined course of events often held to be an irresistible power. I have often wondered if a person's life follows a path that is laid out long before he or she ever takes a first step. Or are we in control of what happens to us?

My name is Kate Worthington and I am a paramedic. I've seen some dramatic events in my life. I've watched people fight to survive, with impressive fortitude, and I've watched others surrender to death peacefully without fear of what lay beyond. Perhaps they could see what waited for them on the other side. Perhaps they knew it was beautiful.

Or perhaps they simply had no notion that they were in any danger to begin with, and simply allowed themselves to be carried along by fate.

I've also seen people come back from the dead, in more ways than one, and I wonder if they returned because there was some unfinished business to attend to. Maybe they still had lessons to learn.

I certainly have more than a few lessons to learn, but I do know one thing: Sometimes life is cruel, and at times it can seem rather pointless and tragic. But occasionally and surprisingly, certain hardships can lead us down a new path we never could have imagined.

And maybe that new path — that unexpected set of changed circumstances — was our destiny all along.

CHAPTER

One

⌾⌾

Saving Lives

I'm sure if you look back, you are able to pinpoint specific
events in your life that changed you forever. For me, one of
those events occurred on a country road in New Hampshire,
in the frigid cold of a mid-February afternoon in 2007, when I
watched a scuba diver pull a dead woman from the bottom of a
frozen lake.

"What happened?" I asked the cop when I stepped out of
the ambulance and felt the heel of my boot slip on a patch of
black ice. "*Whoa.*" I grabbed hold of the side mirror to steady
myself.

"The driver swerved to avoid hitting a deer," he replied, blowing into his hands and rubbing them together to warm them.
"Must have hit the brakes too hard. According to witnesses, the
vehicle did a one-eighty, then rolled down the embankment.
Landed upside down on the ice and stayed there for a minute or
two before the ice broke. Then…down she went."

There were a few cars parked on the side of the road with
their hazard lights blinking. It was the usual scene. Spectators
stood around, watching the show. Cop cars were positioned with
red and blue lights flashing, and other officers in neon yellow
vests waved at oncoming cars, motioning for everyone to move
along.

"How long has the vehicle been underwater?" I asked, not knowing if it was a single driver or an entire family with kids. Heaven forbid.

"About twenty minutes," the cop said. "Lucky thing there was a car following behind. Saw the whole thing and called it in."

"I don't know if I'd call any of this lucky," I said. "How did you get a diver down here so fast?"

"Another stroke of luck," the cop replied. "He's a volunteer with search and rescue, and conveniently, he lives right there." He pointed at a small lakeside bungalow.

"I suppose that *is* lucky."

"Yeah, though I'm not sure how much good it'll do. Twenty minutes under water. I'm not holding out much hope."

I strode closer to the edge of the road to get a better view just as the scuba diver re-surfaced. He bobbed like a cork out of a gaping black hole in the ice.

In his arms, he held the limp body of a woman.

I became a paramedic because I was fascinated by emergency medicine. This obsession began when I was sixteen. How exhilarating to imagine that I could actually save a life. I did briefly consider going to medical school, but didn't feel I had the grades.

Not that it doesn't take brains to be a paramedic. I studied hard to get through the program. On top of that, it takes a certain type of person to keep a cool head in out-of-control situations when people are covered in blood.

I'm proud of my skills. I'm also proud of the fact that I graduated from high school at all, when someone else in my situation might never have made it. I'll explain more about that later, but for now, let's focus on the dead woman.

As soon as the rescue team reached the snow-covered shoreline and set the body down, I checked for a pulse. There wasn't one.

"Hurry," I said. "We have to get her out of here."

I climbed up the embankment, reaching hand over hand, slipping on snow-covered rocks, while the rescue team followed behind me, awkwardly hoisting the gurney. They reached the road at last and extended the wheels. My partner, Bill, bagged and masked the woman while I began chest compressions, which I performed while walking alongside the rolling gurney as we wheeled her to the ambulance.

Bill always did the driving. He enjoyed blasting the horn, running traffic lights, and I'm pretty sure he entered this line of work because he loved the wail of the siren. Me...I always reminded him to slow down and drive with care. All I wanted was to keep my patients safe and tell them everything was going to be okay.

I knew this woman couldn't hear me, but when we slid her into the back of the ambulance and the doors slammed shut, I spoke the words to her regardless. "Everything's going to be okay," I said. Habit I guess.

"Buckled in?" Bill asked over his shoulder as he turned the key in the ignition. He was joking of course, because I had work to do in the back. I was busy putting the leads on and calling ahead to the hospital.

When I had the doctor on the line, I calmly and quickly explained the situation while looking down at the woman's face behind the oxygen mask. She was about my age, mid- to late-thirties, with dark auburn hair. Some of the ends were white with frost. She was a sickly blue-gray color, like a cadaver in a morgue, but also severely hypothermic. That observation gave me hope.

"What's her temperature?" the doc asked me.

I reached into my bag for the digital thermometer. "Eighty-one degrees. And she's soaking wet."

He paused, but only for a second, then began spouting off instructions. "Get her clothes off right away and cover her with a heating blanket. Tell your driver to crank up the heat in the ambulance as high as it will go. Start warm IV fluids. Stick the IV bags down your own shirt if you have to. The goal is to get her warm, even if you can only raise her temperature a few degrees. Don't defibrillate. Not yet. Focus on warming her up to at least eighty-six, then start CPR. We'll be waiting for you outside the ER doors."

I proceeded to remove the patient's wet clothes, then I wrapped her in an electric heating blanket and stuffed the IV bags down my shirt like the doctor suggested.

"Where's a microwave when you need one?" I said to Bill, shocked by the chilly bag against my skin. "Ooh, that's cold."

I couldn't imagine what it had been like for this poor woman, when gallons of ice water came pouring into her car.

I used my stethoscope to check for a heartbeat and looked at her face again. Would we be able to revive her? I wondered. And if we did, would she ever be the same?

"How you doing back there?" Bill asked as he took a hard right turn. I fell forward slightly, then tucked the blanket around the woman a little more tightly.

"We're okay. Do you have the heat up as high as it'll go?"

"Yeah, but do you really think there's any hope? She was down there a long time."

"She's not dead until she's warm and dead," I replied, taking her temperature again. Eighty-three degrees.

"Realistically, how often do they come back without any brain damage?" Bill asked.

"I don't know the stats, but I've seen it happen. When I was a kid, my dad took our dog hunting for rabbits one winter and accidentally shot her."

"Geez," Bill said.

"Dad didn't know that he shot her. He thought she ran off after something, then he found her in the snow after a couple of hours. I don't know how long she was dead, but we all got the shock of our lives when she woke up after my dad brought her home and laid her down by the woodstove."

"Are you sure she was really dead?"

"Yeah, a hundred percent sure. My head was resting on her chest. Maybe it was my body heat that brought her back."

"Sounds like a miracle to me."

I used my stethoscope to listen for a heartbeat again, but still, there was nothing.

"I don't believe in miracles," I said. "It's just science. No different from a frozen dinner that sits in the freezer for six months, then tastes great after five minutes in the microwave."

It was getting warm in the ambulance. I had to unbutton my jacket and shrug out of it. "How much further?" I asked Bill.

"We're five minutes away." He slammed on the brakes and laid on the horn. "Pull over you idiot!" Then he swerved and hit the gas.

I checked the woman's temperature again. It was eighty-six degrees, so I began CPR.

The ambulance doors flew open. I was dripping with sweat. Doctors and nurses surrounded us. Within moments, the woman was wheeled into the trauma room and the doctor yelled, "*Clear!*"

Bill and I backed out at that point, and I exhaled sharply, knowing it would take some time for my adrenaline to slow down. I was wired.

While I went to the tech room to type up my report, Bill offered to fetch me a cup of coffee, but I asked for a cold bottle of Gatorade instead because I felt like I'd just pumped iron in a sauna.

By the time I finished my report, our shift was at an end, but I made sure to check on the woman before I left. "Did they get her back?" I asked the clerk at the nurse's station.

"Yeah, they did. I was surprised because she was down for so long, but Dr. Newman just wouldn't give up. He kept checking her temperature and shocking her, then lo and behold, the heart monitor started beeping. You didn't hear everybody cheering?"

"No."

"Well, there were a few whoops and hollers. It really makes you think. Good job, by the way."

I moved behind the desk to toss my empty Gatorade bottle into the recycling bin, then went to the trauma room. It was empty. They must have taken the woman upstairs.

"Did she say anything when she came to?" I asked, because I couldn't seem to forget the blue pallor of her skin in my ambulance. It was like undressing a corpse. Which I suppose…she was at the time.

"No," the clerk replied, "'cause she didn't actually wake up. She's in a coma. They took her to ICU about ten minutes ago."

The hope and satisfaction I felt was immediately curtailed.

Maybe there was nothing to celebrate after all. Maybe it was just a matter of time before someone would have to pull a plug.

I wondered about her family. Did she have a husband? Children?

As I walked out of the hospital, a sudden wave of exhaustion washed over me. It's not easy to do chest compressions for extended periods of time, and I'd really wanted to bring this woman back. There were moments in the ambulance when I could almost hear her pleading with me to stay hopeful. *Don't…give…up.*

I unlocked my car and climbed into the driver's seat, then sat for a moment with my hands on the steering wheel. Staring straight ahead, I wondered if that voice in my head had less to do with saving that woman's life, and more to do with saving my own.

The COLOR of HOPE

Book Three
Available Now

Diana Moore has led a charmed life. She's the daughter of a wealthy senator and living a glamorous city life, and is confident her handsome live-in boyfriend is about to propose. But everything is turned upside down when she learns of a mysterious woman who works nearby – a woman who is her identical mirror image.

Diana is compelled to discover the truth about this woman's identity, but the truth leads her down a path of secrets, betrayals, and shocking discoveries about her past. These discoveries follow her like a shadow.

Then she meets Dr. Jacob Peterson—a brilliant cardiac surgeon with an uncanny ability to heal those who are broken. With his help, Diana embarks upon a journey to restore her belief in the human spirit, and recover a sense of hope - that happiness, and love, may still be within reach for those willing to believe in second chances.

The COLOR of A DREAM

Book Four
Available Now

Nadia Carmichael has had a lifelong run of bad luck. It begins on the day she is born, when she is separated from her identical twin sister and put up for adoption. Twenty-seven years later, not long after she is finally reunited with her twin and is expecting her first child, Nadia falls victim to a mysterious virus and requires a heart transplant.

Now recovering from the surgery with a new heart, Nadia is haunted by a recurring dream that sets her on a path to discover the identity of her donor. Her efforts are thwarted, however, when the father of her baby returns to sue for custody of their child. It's not until Nadia learns of his estranged brother Jesse that she begins to explore the true nature of her dreams, and discover what her new heart truly needs and desires...

The COLOR *of*
A MEMORY

Book Five
Available Now

ER nurse Audrey Fitzgerald believed she was married to the perfect man - a heroic firefighter who saved lives, even beyond his own death. But a year after losing him she meets a mysterious woman who has some unexplained connection to her husband...

Soon Audrey discovers that in the weeks leading up to her husband's death, he was keeping secrets, and she wonders if she ever really knew him at all. Compelled to dig into his past and explore memories that define the essence of their relationship, Audrey embarks upon a journey of discovery that will lead her down a new path to the future - a future she never dared to imagine.

The COLOR of LOVE

Book Six
Available August 2014

Carla Matthews is a single mother struggling to make ends meet and give her daughter Kaleigh a decent upbringing. When Kaleigh's absent father Seth—a famous alpine climber who never wanted to be tied down—begs for a second chance at fatherhood, Carla is hesitant because she doesn't want to pin her hopes on a man who is always seeking another mountain to scale. A man who was never willing to stay put in one place and raise a family.

But when Seth's plane goes missing after a crash landing in the harsh Canadian wilderness, Carla must wait for news…Is he dead or alive? Will the wreckage ever be found?

One year later, after having given up all hope, Carla receives a phone call that shocks her to her core. A man has been found, half-dead, floating on an iceberg in the North Atlantic, uttering her name. Is this Seth? And is it possible that he will come home to her and Kaleigh at last, and be the man she always dreamed he would be?

The Color of the Season: Book Seven
Availailable November 2014

The Color of Joy: Book Eight
Available February 2015

Praise for Julianne MacLean's
bestselling romances...

"You can always count on Julianne MacLean to deliver ravishing romance that will keep you turning pages until the wee hours of the morning."

—Teresa Medeiros

"She is just an all-around, wonderful writer and I look forward to reading everything she writes."

—*Romance Junkies*

"Julianne MacLean knows what her audience likes…compelling characters and a soul-baring journey of love."

—*ReadertoReader.com*

"MacLean's compelling writing turns this simple, classic love story into a richly emotional romance, and by combining engaging characters with a unique, vividly detailed setting, she has created an exceptional tale for readers who hunger for something a bit different in their historical romances."

—*Booklist*

About the Author

Julianne MacLean is a *USA Today* bestselling author of many historical romances, including The Highlander Series with St. Martin's Press and her popular American Heiress Series with Avon/Harper Collins. She also writes contemporary mainstream fiction, and *The Color of Heaven* was a *USA Today* bestseller. She is a three-time RITA finalist, and has won numerous awards, including the Booksellers' Best Award, the Book Buyer's Best Award, and a Reviewers' Choice Award from Romantic Times for Best Regency Historical of 2005. She lives in Nova Scotia with her husband and daughter, and is a dedicated member of Romance Writers of Atlantic Canada. Please visit Julianne's website for more information about her books and writing life, and while you're there, be sure to sign up for her reader newsletter to stay informed about upcoming books and special events.

Other Books by
Julianne MacLean

The American Heiress Series
To Marry the Duke
An Affair Most Wicked
My Own Private Hero
Love According to Lily
Portrait of a Lover
Surrender to a Scoundrel

The Pembroke Palace Series
In My Wildest Fantasies
The Mistress Diaries
When a Stranger Loves Me
Married By Midnight
A Kiss Before the Wedding - A Pembroke Palace Short Story
Seduced at Sunset

The Highlander Trilogy
Captured by the Highlander
Claimed by the Highlander
Seduced by the Highlander
The Rebel – A Highland Short Story

The Royal Trilogy
Be My Prince
Princess in Love
The Prince's Bride

Harlequin Historical Romances
Prairie Bride
The Marshal and Mrs. O'Malley
Adam's Promise

Time Travel Romance
Taken by the Cowboy

The Color of Heaven Series
The Color of Heaven
The Color of Destiny
The Color of Hope
The Color of a Dream
The Color of a Memory
The Color of Love
The Color of Joy

Please visit the author's website for information about other new releases in this series as they become available.

The Color of Heaven series books are also available as audiobooks.

Made in the USA
San Bernardino, CA
10 March 2020

65513180R00183